DEVOURING

THE BOY'S FACE TWISTED INTO SOMETHING
INHUMAN — VICIOUS, PITILESS. ITS SOOTY MAW
OPENED, TENDRILS OF SMOKE WAFTED OUT LIKE
VIPERS, AND A DEEP INHUMAN VOICE CALLED TO THEM.
"LET . . . ME . . . OUT."

Look out for the second soul-sucking book
in this terrifying series.

THE DEVOURING

SIMON HOLT

PUFFIN

PUFFIN BOOKS

Published by the Penguin Group
Penguin Books Ltd, 80 Strand, London WC2R 0RL, England
Penguin Group (USA) Inc., 375 Hudson Street, New York, New York 10014, USA
Penguin Group (Canada), 90 Eglinton Avenue East, Suite 700, Toronto, Ontario, Canada M4P 2Y3
(a division of Pearson Penguin Canada Inc.)
Penguin Ireland, 25 St Stephen's Green, Dublin 2, Ireland (a division of Penguin Books Ltd)
Penguin Group (Australia), 250 Camberwell Road, Camberwell, Victoria 3124, Australia
(a division of Pearson Australia Group Pty Ltd)
Penguin Books India Pvt Ltd, 11 Community Centre, Panchsheel Park, New Delhi – 110 017, India
Penguin Group (NZ), 67 Apollo Drive, Rosedale, North Shore 0632, New Zealand
(a division of Pearson New Zealand Ltd)
Penguin Books (South Africa) (Pty) Ltd, 24 Sturdee Avenue, Rosebank, Johannesburg 2196, South Africa

Penguin Books Ltd, Registered Offices: 80 Strand, London WC2R 0RL, England

puffinbooks.com

First published in the USA by Little, Brown and Company (Hachette Book Group USA) 2008
Published in Great Britain in Puffin Books 2008
1

Copyright © 2008 by Star Farm Productions LLC
Based upon an original idea by Mark Allen Smith
All rights reserved

The moral right of the author has been asserted

Set in Adobe Caslon
Made and printed in England by Clays Ltd, St Ives plc

British Library Cataloguing in Publication Data
A CIP catalogue record for this book is available from the British Library

ISBN: 978-0-141-32526-2

www.greenpenguin.co.uk

Penguin Books is committed to a sustainable future
for our business, our readers and our planet.
The book in your hands is made from paper
certified by the Forest Stewardship Council.

TO CARY, CATHY, CONNIE AND ALVINA

PROLOGUE

On Sorry Night, just a few days before Christmas, you have to snuff the lamps, douse the flames in the fireplace and spend the night in the cold and dark. If you don't, the Vours will get you.

They're the monsters you can't see, the ones that crave the heat and light. The ones that feed on your fear and then swallow you whole. I should know. When I was a child, I saw it happen, and I've lived with that fear ever since.

That night, Jeremiah and I came in the back door just after sunset, chased by a cold December wind. Pa stood at the window with his back to us, clenching his mug and gazing out into the snowy night. I knew we were in trouble when I saw the whiskey bottle on the kitchen table.

'You remember to bring them cows in?'

Pa was a giant in thick boots and faded overalls. I shivered as he turned to face us. His eyes were empty and cold like the winter fields outside, and just as dead. He got like that when he drank. I think that after Ma died, some part of him did too.

I saw the colour run right out of Jeremiah's cheeks. 'Oh, I – I forgot, Pa.'

He smiled at me, but I knew he was afraid. It was my fault.

I'd begged for a piggyback ride before the sun went down, and before the chores were done. That was why he'd forgotten to put the cows in the barn.

'You got straw for brains?'

'No, Pa.'

'I think maybe you do. I think we best find a job a boy with straw for brains can do.'

Pa slammed his mug down so hard the whiskey splashed out of it. He dragged Jeremiah out of the door by the arm, grabbing a rope and lantern from a hook outside as they headed for the cornfield. I followed, running and slipping on icy mud in the dark.

Pa strode up to the old scarecrow that loomed on its cross over the field. With one yank, he ripped it from its nails. Then he tore off the head and threw the body to the ground. Pa looked like some kind of fairy-book monster, holding up that burlap head in his giant fist. He threw it at Jeremiah's feet.

'See there? Straw for brains, just like you. Now get up on that post, boy – you're gonna do yourself some scarecrowing.'

Jeremiah's breath came in sharp bursts of steam.

'But – but, Pa, there ain't no corn. It's the winter.'

'No corn, no crows. So it'll be an easy job, won't it?'

Pa thrust Jeremiah up against the post. Then he snatched one of my brother's wrists and lashed it to the crossbeam with the rope. Tears streaked down Jeremiah's face as Pa tied down the other one.

I cried for my brother too. Even though he was ten years old, four years older than me, he was still scared of the dark. He said he could feel monsters in the night, waiting in the shadows to come and get him. He called them the Vours.

2

It was a story that has been passed from kid to kid since who knows when. Ma used to tell us it was probably some old Indian nonsense, nothing to worry about. Pa, he'd just say, 'You only have to worry about them taking your soul one night a year – Sorry Night. The longest, darkest night of the year.' And then he'd laugh.

Pa lit the lantern and put it down beside the post.

'Pa, please.' My brother's voice shuddered and his body shook. 'Not tonight. Any night but tonight.'

'How long does Jeremiah have to stay out here?' I asked.

'Till it's done.'

And then my father made me leave my brother tied up in the freezing black air. I looked back over my shoulder at Jeremiah. His coat had fallen open by his throat, and the St Giles medal he always wore gleamed in the lantern light. I silently prayed for St Giles to protect Jeremiah's soul from the monsters.

Pa sent me to bed, but I wouldn't sleep, and after a while I sneaked back into the kitchen. Pa was passed out, face down at the table, the empty whiskey bottle turned on its side. I threw on my coat over my nightgown, pulled on my big boots and ran to the cornfield.

The lantern cast a flickering circle of light at Jeremiah's feet. It reflected on his St Giles medal, which shone like a heart on fire at the centre of a dark cross. I dashed up to him and threw my arms round his neck, my tears wetting his frozen skin. His teeth chattered behind his lips, and ice frosted his eyelashes.

'It's coming.'

'I'm here,' I said, struggling to untie the knots round his wrist. But the rope was so tight, and my fingers were numb.

'Can you see it? The shadow – moving! Coming for me!'

3

I looked around, but all I could see was the flickering lantern, the black shapes of the barn and the house, and endless fields of white. The wind moaned.

'It's just me, Jeremiah. I'll get you down.' I pleaded with him, but he kept screaming.

'Get it away!'

Suddenly the lantern flared up, white-hot, and the glass shattered. I cried out and covered my head as kerosene spattered over the snow, flames snapping up at the air around us. The headless scarecrow on the ground caught fire and crackled as it burned. A billowing pillar of smoke rose up like a giant black snake, coiling round my brother up on the cross.

God forgive me, I ran. I ran as fast as I could, the cold burning in my lungs, Jeremiah's screams burning in my ears. I didn't save him. I didn't bring him back.

This isn't how the horror ended for us – this is how it began.

As I ran, the screaming suddenly stopped, and I heard something much worse. It was Jeremiah's voice, but different, lower, resonating across the field like a demon's olden chant:

When dark creeps in and eats the light,
Bury your fears on Sorry Night.
For in the winter's blackest hours
Comes the feasting of the Vours.
No one can see it, the life they stole,
Your body's here but not your soul . . .

1

'Stop, Reggie!' Henry barked from beneath his quilt. 'Don't read any more!'

Regina Halloway shut the book.

Since Mom had left them without so much as a goodbye kiss almost a year ago, taking only a packed suitcase and a photo album, Reggie had been forced to assume a number of extra duties around the house. With school, friends and a job to worry about, a large portion of those duties – laundry, vacuuming, dishes – went undone for extended periods until Dad cracked the whip. Bedtime-story duty, however, was never overlooked.

But she'd quickly grown tired of the usual kiddie fare and had decided to introduce Henry to some juicier stuff. And, to Reggie, juicier meant scary.

'You said you weren't going to get scared.'

The lump beside her shuddered.

'Did the Vours really get Jeremiah?' it whispered.

'Of course not. It's just a story, Henry.'

'But tomorrow is December twenty-second, Reggie. Tomorrow night is Sorry Night!'

Reggie pulled the covers down to reveal a wide-eyed eight-year-old boy with wild curls, clutching a stuffed koala.

'I knew you wouldn't be able to handle it.' She tried to stand up but he clutched her arm. 'Go to sleep, Hen.'

'Wait!' Henry scrunched his skinny body against her. 'Don't leave.'

He reminded Reggie of a newborn in an *Animal Planet* documentary, burrowing into its mother for warmth. The two of them had been close, even with the seven-year age gap, but things were different now. Now he reached for her hand more often, leaned against her on the couch watching TV, and wandered into her room after dinner with nothing more to say than 'Hi'. He wasn't growing up; he was reverting to a small, frightened child. And his clinginess was suffocating her.

Henry reached out a hand and traced his fingers across the book's cracked, brown leather cover. It was an old journal Reggie had found in one of the shipping boxes she'd unpacked at her part-time job at the used bookstore. *The Devouring* had been splayed across the first page in slanting, spidery handwriting, like a title page to a novel. Intrigued, she had slid it into her backpack. When she was done reading it, she'd just stick it in with the next shipment. No harm done.

Reggie discovered the book contained a bizarre, handwritten narrative of monsters called 'Vours' that could take over people's bodies and minds when they were most frightened. But, according to the author, they could only do this one night a year, on Sorry Night, the night of the winter solstice. Reggie wondered if this was an author's first draft of a novel, but an online search

6

turned up nothing to suggest that a book called *The Devouring* had ever been published.

The journal was dense; shaky handwriting and rambling narratives made some sections painfully hard to read. Creepy sketches and symbols adorned its yellowed pages at odd intervals, but Reggie could find no method to the author's madness. Part ghost story, part kabbalistic research and part frenzied ravings, the book both captivated and disturbed her.

'I don't like being scared, Reg. I thought maybe –'

Reggie stroked her brother's warm cheek and offered him a tired smile. 'Then no more scary stories, okay?'

Henry nodded. In his cage across the room, General Squeak, Henry's hamster, ran round and round in his plastic wheel.

'Why do you like being scared, Reg?' Henry yawned.

'No more questions. If you're still awake when Dad gets home, we'll *both* have something to be scared about.'

'Please, just answer this one?'

Reggie considered the question.

'Well, I guess the short answer is, it's good practice.'

'*Practice?* For what?'

'For when you're *really* scared.'

'Being scared is practice for being scared?' Henry's eyes closed. He was starting to drift off. 'I don't get it.'

'Think of it this way,' Reggie said. 'If you don't learn how to be scared, you'll never really learn how to be brave.' She swung her feet off the bed and Henry grabbed her arm again.

'Stay till I fall asleep. Don't leave me alone.'

Reggie sighed and sat back on the bed.

General Squeak finished his marathon, and soon the only sound was Henry's breathing. She kissed her sleeping brother on the forehead.

'You're not alone, Henry,' she said softly. 'I'm here.'

2

Sometime during the night, four inches of fresh snow fell on the small town of Cutter's Wedge. Walking to school, Henry couldn't get enough of it – running through it, jumping in it, kicking at it. He'd pestered Dad for rides out to the slopes to snowboard every weekend, and would keep it up until spring. Reggie and her best friend, Aaron Cole, watched him race around like a puppy off a leash.

Aaron wore a fedora tilted at a jaunty angle, but his hat was the least of his eccentricities. His love of B-grade horror films, his encyclopedic knowledge of serial killers and his preoccupation with government conspiracies all pushed him beyond geeky and into the realm of the truly strange.

'Henry,' Reggie hollered, 'you get soaked and you'll freeze your butt off in class!'

Aaron rolled his eyes.

'Could you possibly be a bigger bummer?'

Reggie frowned.

'Did I really say that?'

Aaron summoned his best shlockmeister impression.

'Coming soon! The new novel from horror master Stephen

King: *Regina*! The bloodcurdling tale of a small-town teen who wakes up one morning to discover . . . *she has become her brother's mother*!'

A snowball splatted against Aaron's hat, sending it flying off of his head.

'Bullseye! You're dead, punk!' Henry crowed, standing six metres away, moulding another snowball.

Aaron picked up his hat and dusted the snow off.

'*Au contraire!* You messed with my *hat*, which means *you're* dead!'

He handed the hat to Reggie and took off for Henry, who turned tail and ran. 'Graceful' was never a word Reggie would use to describe Aaron. His long legs always seemed to be trying to catch up to each other, and his arms did more flapping than pumping. Aaron's brain was a finely tuned machine, and its only real issue was coordinating with his body. Still, he had no trouble catching eight-year-old Henry. He swept him up from behind and they both tumbled into the snow, laughing and wrestling. Reggie came and stood over them.

'Don't hurt him,' she said.

'I won't,' said Aaron.

'I was talking to Henry.'

Henry let loose with a flurry of kung-fu chops and battle cries, and Aaron covered his head in mock fright.

'I give! I give!'

'Don't mess with the best!' Henry hopped to his feet, triumphant.

He ran towards the red-brick primary school and joined the stream of kids pouring in. As Aaron got to his feet, Reggie brushed the snow off him and handed back his hat. He put it on and the two of them headed across the street to Cutter High.

The quad was crammed with sleepy teenagers in their usual state of semi-android techno-consciousness, leaning on the walls and squatting on the stairs. They were isolated by headphones, entranced by cell phones, tapping on laptops and mutely communing with the WiFi spirit world. The four-storey stone relic of a school loomed over it all. Reggie always expected to see an Igor incarnation peering down at her from the rooftop, a squawking raven perched on his shoulder.

Reggie and Aaron were neither popular nor unpopular. They were part of the group Aaron called the *heynodders* – those whose social standing meant that if they made random eye contact with someone in the hall, they'd probably get a nod back, and maybe even a quick 'Hey'. They both had their share of friends – kids they could hang with at their lockers or the lunchroom – but the exchanges were mostly teenage business-as-usual: music, TV and movie critiques, where who bought what, and news flashes about hook-ups and broken hearts.

As Aaron and Reggie climbed the steps to head into school, the Kassner twins stepped from the crowd and blocked the doors. The two wore hooded sweatshirts under black field jackets, filthy jeans and steel-toed boots. They looked like thugs with shaved heads and broad chests. Keech rarely spoke, Mitch never did and neither seemed interested in anything other than destruction.

But the Kassners' size and aggression, while daunting to most of the student body, was a boon to the football coach, who immediately recruited them to play right and left tackle. This status seemed to give them permission to pick on anybody they wanted to, and they did. Aaron was a favourite target, ever since he'd made a sarcastic comment about the twins' Cro-Magnon looks in world history and word got back to them.

Keech grabbed the fedora off Aaron's head. 'You think this makes you look tough, Cole? Like a gangster?'

Aaron just looked at the ground.

'Taking someone's hat? Really? Is that it?' Reggie glared at them and stepped forward. 'You'd think with such a fat head you'd have more brains in there.' The twins intimidated the hell out of her, but she'd never let them know that.

Keech held the hat out towards Reggie. She grabbed at it, but he pulled it away again and crammed it on his own bald head.

The first-period bell rang, and the quad's sea of bodies started flowing towards the school's entrance. Keech turned with Mitch and headed into the school.

'Thanks for trying,' said Aaron as he and Reggie shuffled off to class. 'God, I need to grow a pair.'

'They're just assholes, Aaron. Don't let them get to you.'

As they made their way through the crowds, a voice rang out from behind them.

'Keech!'

The brute jock turned round.

Reggie looked over her shoulder to see Quinn Waters, a junior as much renowned for his athletic prowess as his dimples, making his way towards them with a confident strut and easy smile. Tall and lean, with dark curls, he was the best quarterback in Cutter High history, an upperclassman god in a rugby shirt.

'Hat!' he called down the corridor.

Keech stared at him for a moment before the hat came sailing over the crowd. Quinn caught it with one hand and gave it back to Aaron.

'Sorry about that, man. I'd kill them myself if they didn't keep me so damn snug in the pocket.'

Aaron looked at Reggie, who seemed to be under some sort of Quinn trance, staring at him with her mouth slightly open. He leaned towards her as he dug around in his backpack.

'This is business,' he whispered. 'Try not to drool.'

Like I'd even have a chance with him, she thought. Quinn was an A-list guy, and he went out with A-list girls. It wasn't that she thought of herself as some sort of cow or freak, but she just wasn't much of anybody. If Cutter High were a movie, Reggie Halloway would be an extra. She wore T-shirts or plain, solid-coloured sweaters, jeans and sneakers or army surplus boots. Reggie considered her best feature to be her long, dark hair, the colour of rich chocolate – but because she had to make the family breakfast and take care of Henry every morning, she never had time to style it. More often than not, it was tied back into a long, frizzy ponytail. Make-up usually was at a minimum too. Her eyes were dark and shining, though. Aaron said they were 'vampish'; she guessed that was a pretty high compliment coming from him, but doubted that was Quinn's taste.

Aaron had dug a Manila folder from his book bag. He glanced around furtively as Quinn handed him a fifty-dollar bill in exchange for the folder. Quinn eyed the pristine five-page paper inside.

'"Hamlet's Dilemma." Good for a B plus?'

'Yup.'

'Sweet.'

Aaron had started 'the business' two years ago. At first, it had been tricky – finding the right voice to write papers that read like something a guy like Quinn would hand in, only a little better. Reggie considered it unethical, immoral and illegal. Aaron agreed and looked at it as valuable preparation for the real world.

Aaron pocketed his fee and started to leave.

Quinn looked up.

'Wait a sec. Tell me what –'

'Sorry – three more deliveries.' Aaron winked at Reggie.

Aaron disappeared into the crowd, leaving the two of them standing together. As people passed by, it seemed as if every other student said 'Hey, Quinn,' or 'What's up, Q?' Reggie wondered what it was like to have to say 'Hello' back to a hundred people a day.

Quinn studied Reggie for a moment before saying, 'Halloway, right?'

Reggie was stunned. He knew her name?

'Uh-huh,' she said.

'Freshman?' Quinn asked. 'I think you're in my study hall.'

'Uh-huh,' Reggie said, successfully executing another nod. She *was* in his study hall, but she hadn't thought his field of vision extended to the table in the back where she sat.

Quinn had turned his attention back to the paper. He flipped through it and frowned. Reggie didn't think she'd ever seen him without his faint, cool smile. They were almost alone now in the hallway. Somehow, it made her a little braver.

Quinn's pale green eyes studied her. He unwrapped a stick of gum, popped it in his mouth and chewed nervously.

'I've got English first period – right now – and . . .'

'You didn't read the play?'

Quinn shrugged and smiled at her. But it was different from his perfect smile. It was wistful, and a little crooked. Right then, Reggie realized she was witness to a historic event. Quinn Waters was human. Imperfect. Uncertain, even. It was almost as if she were seeing a stage actor slip out of character for a second.

'Don't get the wrong impression, okay? I started the play, dug the whole father's ghost thing, but then I got slammed . . .'

His closeness made Reggie's pulse quicken. He smelled really good.

'Teachers love to pour it on before break. Some sort of code,' she said, slumping melodramatically under the weight of her satchel. The shoulder strap ripped, and Reggie's books and binders spilled all over the floor.

'Damn it!' Her face reddened, and she wished she could climb into her emptied bag and hide there. And just when she had started speaking like a functioning person too.

She knelt on the ground and began shoving the books back into her bag. Quinn bent down to help her and picked up the journal before she could stop him.

'What's *The Devouring*?' he asked, examining it curiously.

'Huh? Oh, that. Just some monster story. Written like a journal. I collect . . .' She was nerding out and couldn't stop. 'I'm a horror fan and I collect stuff like that – scary stories and stuff. I know. I'm a total geek.'

15

Quinn helped Reggie to her feet. 'No, no. Not at all. That's cool. Very.' He handed the journal back to her.

'Cool? Very?' She raised an eyebrow at him.

'You got me. You are a geek.' Quinn laughed and ran his fingers through his hair. 'But not a total geek – total geeks aren't usually cute.'

He stopped abruptly, as if he couldn't believe he'd just said that out loud. Reggie felt her cheeks burn.

'So, um, Hamlet,' she said.

'Right! Hamlet!'

'The nutshell: he knows his uncle killed his father and waffles about whether or not he should take revenge.'

'Does he? Take revenge?'

'Yeah, but he's too late. He poisons his uncle but then –'

'He dies, right?'

'Everyone dies in Shakespeare.'

'Sweet.' Quinn glanced around the empty hall. 'Late for class. Gotta go turn in my paper. Thanks for the help.'

Reggie stared up at him like a puppy dog. 'You're welcome.'

Quinn walked a few steps but looked back at her to say, 'See you in study hall. I'll save you a seat.'

She nodded, not entirely believing what had just happened.

3

The wind, like a stranger demanding entry, rattled the window shutters of Reggie's bedroom. She lay on top of her bed's quilt, absently flipping through an old *Vault of Horror* comic. Aaron sat cross-legged on the floor nearby, reading aloud from *The Devouring*.

> *They lurk in the cold and dark. Hungry and wicked, they wait for their one chance to devour the weak on Sorry Night. Then the Vours feast on a banquet of fear. Your fear. They steal your soul but your body remains. No one knows the difference.*

He looked up at Reggie. 'Whoever wrote this journal was clearly insane.'

'You love that stuff.' She tossed the comic book aside.

'Oh, hell yeah!' Aaron laughed. 'Ever since you let me borrow it, I can't get it out of my head. So, are we still going to give the Vours a call tonight, Bloody Mary-style?'

17

'If you brought the supplies, sure.' She grinned. 'We have to terrify ourselves. That's how they got Jeremiah.'

'So if I get devoured, will you come save me?'

'Not a chance.' Reggie took a lighter from her pocket and then lit the three black candles on her nightstand. She switched off the bedside lamp. 'You ready to *face your fear*?'

'God, we're über-geeks,' Aaron said. Shadows cast in the flickering candlelight cavorted across the wall behind him. 'First night of vacation, other kids party, but we –'

'What's with the candles?'

Henry stood in the doorway, scratching his pyjama-clad butt. Reggie frowned.

'You're supposed to be sleeping.'

He yawned before saying, 'Not tired. What're you guys doing, anyway?'

Reggie stood up and pointed to the doorway. 'Go back to bed.'

Beyond the window, a gust of wind howled. The shutters rattled in reply. Henry winced.

'The blizzard's keeping me awake. I should just stay in here.'

'Nice try,' said Reggie. 'Bed. *Now*.'

'But Dad's gone tonight! Who cares?'

When Dad said he was going to be out of town overnight bidding on contracts, she knew that it wouldn't mean more freedom, but less. Most kids would see it as a chance to have a house party, but for Reggie it meant an unpaid babysitting gig.

She stood up and loomed over her brother. '*Go*.'

Henry hung his head.

'Fine,' he said.

'Night, Henry,' said Aaron.

'Night.'

'Come on. I'll tuck you back in.'

They walked back to his room, and Henry squealed when Reggie snatched him up and flipped him onto his bed. He wriggled under the covers.

'What are you and Aaron going to do?'

'None of your business,' she said as she walked towards the door.

'Wait! What if I have nightmares?'

'Is this still about the Vours? Henry, they're not real.'

'But tonight's Sorry Night!'

Reggie sat down on the bed.

'Listen, if you get scared, close your eyes and think of something really good. A good time you had, or a favourite place, or somebody you love. You'll be asleep before you know it – and it's a hundred per cent nightmare-proof. Okay?'

'Okay.'

Henry kissed his sister on the cheek and lay back, pulling the covers up to his chin.

'Goodnight, Reg.'

'Goodnight. Sweet dreams.'

When Reggie walked back to her room, it felt colder. Aaron looked ghoulish in the candlelight; his face seemed waxy, and shadows filled his eye sockets. Her heart quickened when he pulled a jar from the backpack beside him. A dark shape crawled about inside it.

'He okay?' Aaron asked.

'Henry? He's fine. Just a little spooked by the story.'

'Me too.' He lifted the jar to her as if proposing a toast. 'Ready?'

'No. But this is the only night to do it.' Reggie closed her eyes, gritted her teeth and stuck out her hand. The jar lid scraped as Aaron unscrewed it. 'So *do* it.'

Something prickly stepped onto her palm. It moved slowly at first, exploring the hollows of her knuckles as it wandered up her fingers.

Pointy legs skirted over her thumb. Reggie flinched.

'Open your eyes,' said Aaron. 'Face your fear.'

Reggie peeked. The face of her fear was a wolf spider with a swollen body and bristling legs. It was nearly the width of her wrist.

'Oh, God.' Reggie cringed. As if the spider could feel her fear, it scuttled up her arm in a matter of seconds.

'Time?' she demanded.

'Forty-five to go,' said Aaron, glancing at the stopwatch in his hand. 'Forty . . .'

Reggie clenched her eyes shut. She felt the spider crawl up her neck and into her hair, the gorged abdomen dragging across her scalp. Now the crown of her head, then down onto her forehead. Her stomach lurched and her skin crawled, as if both were trying to squirm away from her body.

Its legs brushed past her brows and stopped on the tip of her nose. She wanted to scream, but her throat constricted. All that came out was a weak rattle.

'Five . . . four . . . three . . . two . . . one. Done!' shouted Aaron.

'Get it off! Get it off!' Reggie shrieked, swiping the spider off her nose. It landed on the rug and scrambled off into a corner before Aaron could grab it. Reggie jumped around her room and brushed at her face, still feeling the prickly legs on her cheek.

'Great, now that thing's loose in my room,' she muttered, once she had calmed down a bit.

'It will probably have spider babies in your sock drawer,' said Aaron brightly. 'So, are you a Vour?'

'Don't think so.' Reggie shivered. 'But then again, if I were a Vour, how would you know?'

'This is true.' Aaron poked Reggie's forehead. 'What did you do with my loser friend, you Vour bastard?'

'Still ... hungry ... must ... eat ... more ... fear ...' Reggie grabbed Aaron's wrist and dragged him down the stairs to the back porch, her laughter drowning in the howling wind.

———

Squeak – squeak – squeak.

General Squeak ran round and round in his metal wheel. Sometimes he would skitter about all night, making all sorts of little noises, but Henry liked knowing he had a friend with him in the dark.

Especially tonight.

Outside, the blizzard raged. Gusts of falling snow swirled against the windowpanes like ghosts seeking escape from the cold. The house quaked beneath their wails.

Henry pulled the blanket over his head and covered his ears. Why hadn't he told Reggie to close the blinds? Think of something good. She'd said to think of something good.

Henry closed his eyes and tried to imagine all the things he liked about winter: his snowboard, hot chocolate, Christmas presents, Reggie taking him sledding . . .

Reggie . . . why couldn't he hear her through the vent connecting their rooms?

Another wail, louder this time. Closer. Henry poked his head out from under the covers; his panicked gaze darted around the room.

The blue glow of his penguin night light, usually so comforting, had the opposite effect tonight. Everything looked submerged, crystallized – frozen. Even Kappy the Koala, his favourite stuffed animal, had a sinister air. The koala's deformed shadow, a long inhuman shape lunging across the floor, seemed to be cast by some other malevolent thing.

Henry remembered the story of Jeremiah: how he was left alone on Sorry Night, terrified in the dark, with the glow of a single lantern at his feet. The Vour had come to him like a moth to the flame.

The night light flickered.

When dark creeps in and eats the light . . .

His breath came faster.

Another icy gale howled outside, and the walls shivered around him. The night light flared briefly and then, with a sharp buzzing crackle, it died. Winter night swallowed the room. Henry trembled, alone in the dark.

He crawled out of bed and felt his way to the door.

'Reggie?' he called out.

He opened his door and then crept down the hallway, feeling along the walls. Henry hurried to Reggie's door and pushed it

22

open. Three black candles burned on the nightstand, their flames mere pinpricks of light in an empty room.

'Reggie? Aaron?'

No one answered.

The window's shutters banged and rattled, and a frigid draught snuffed out the candles' meagre light. He ran back to his own bedroom and threw himself into bed, burying himself in blankets. He choked on his breath.

Reggie, Aaron – they were gone.

Bury your fears on Sorry Night . . .

He wanted his mother, but she was gone too.

Think of something good, Reggie had said. A good time you had, or a favourite place, or somebody you love. Henry squeezed his eyes shut and tried to remember the day his family went to the carnival. He thought of cotton candy sweetness dissolving on his tongue, of waving to his parents from the carousel, of winning Kappy the Koala from the water-gun game, of his mother's dark hair shining in the July sunlight . . .

'Why did you leave us?' he whispered, tears nestling in the corners of his lips. 'Come back, Mommy. Please come back.'

Only the weeping wind answered his pleas, flooding him with fear, chilling his thoughts and coagulating into something black and dead – until something alive and hungry pulled him towards sleep.

The snow continued to swirl against the window, but the mournful gusts came less frequently now. The storm was passing. The soft melody of a carnival calliope played in the distance.

For in the winter's darkest hours . . .

The doorknob turned. The bedroom door opened just enough

23

to let in a slant of the dull orange hall light, and a cool draught carried with it the aroma of buttered popcorn and powdered sugar. Henry pulled the covers tightly around him.

'Reggie?'

There was no answer. All was still. Then a figure stood in the doorway. Her long brown curls, wide blue eyes and gleaming white smile all seemed so real and wonderfully alive.

Comes the feasting of the Vours . . .

'Mommy?'

Soundlessly, she crossed the wood floor and sat in her familiar spot on his bed. Her thin, elegant arm reached for the lamp on his nightstand, and the metal chain chinked against the ceramic post.

Henry gazed at his mother's beautiful face in the lamplight. She was here. He wiped his tear-filled eyes.

'Mommy, is it really you?'

'It's me, sweet boy. You called to me and I've come.'

The voice was hers, the face was hers, the hair and the smile and the smell were hers. It was *her*. Henry clutched his mother fiercely, burying his face in her breast. But the deeper he pressed into her, the more he shivered.

No one can see it, the life they stole . . .

'You're cold, Mommy.' Henry sobbed, digging into her clothes, trying to feel the warmth of her body. 'You're so cold.'

'I am, sweetheart. Very cold. But I'll be warm again soon.' She coiled her arms round Henry's quivering body.

The bulb in the lamp faded as a cold wind sighed through the room. Frost spiderwebbed across the window, jagged icy cuts interlacing over blackness.

24

'Am I dreaming, Mom?' He flailed in the wintry darkness, grasping for heat and some small promise of love. 'I don't want to be dreaming. I'm so scared . . .'

'I know. But I'm here with you, Henry. I'll always be here.' Her ivory skin rippled like water, and inky tendrils of cold black smoke oozed from her nostrils and mouth. 'There's nothing to be afraid of.'

Your body's here but not your soul . . .

Henry closed his eyes and let the darkness in.

———◦◦◦———

Reggie dragged the cover off the hot tub on her back deck as Aaron watched. The newly fallen snow's weight made it a more laborious task than usual, but at last it tumbled aside. A billowing cloud of steam rolled from the water's surface and swirled around them. The tub's water heater still worked, but the bubble-jets had failed months ago. It was one of the many things Reggie's dad hadn't had time to fix since her mom had left. In the darkness, the water in the tub seemed black. The whole thing looked like a giant cauldron.

The snowstorm had mostly blown over, but the air remained sharp and dry; the hot tub's steam did nothing to lessen the chill. Overhead, a starless sky closed in the world like a tomb.

'It's freezing out here, Aaron. You sure you want to do this?'

'I'm not chickening out.' He already felt ridiculous, wearing nothing but rubber flip-flops, Hawaiian-print swim trunks and a thick terry-cloth robe of Reggie's. Even though his shivering had little to do with the cold, he wouldn't back down.

'Okay, then. Ready?'

Aaron nodded. He kicked off the flip-flops and shrugged off the robe, hoping the night masked not only his pale body but also his surging terror. If Reggie had let a huge spider crawl on her for one minute, he could stay underwater for just as long. He climbed onto the edge of the tub and plunged in his feet. Its bathwater temperature was much warmer than the air, but gooseflesh crawled across his skin nonetheless. The wet seeped up Aaron's swim trunks as he lowered himself in. Reggie took out the stopwatch.

'You can do it,' she said. She held the watch up. 'Ready . . . and . . . go!'

Aaron took a deep breath and sank into the water.

As it enveloped him, he heard his heart pounding in his ears. The memory of his seventh birthday came surging back: he'd been wading in Noe Lake, searching for crawfish, and had lost his footing on an algae-covered stone at the edge of a steep descent. In a moment he'd slipped into the deeper water; as he thrashed about, he had caught his foot between rocks on the lake's floor. Aaron remembered the panic, water filling his mouth and his nostrils.

He opened his eyes and looked up. Where was Reggie? He couldn't see her. The water was crushing him, seeping in through his ears, his lips, his nose. His lungs burned and his body convulsed. The roar of submersion pounded in his head, and he felt himself spinning. Soon he would involuntarily gasp for air and find none. There was no up or down. There was only the black water. It was deeper than the ocean, darker than the grave. It was stronger than him. It would come rushing in; it would flood his lungs, pressing on him from the inside until he burst.

Panicked and helpless, Aaron opened his mouth and a slug of water filled his throat. He gagged and convulsed in a desperate attempt to draw a breath. But already his body was drowning, bloating, dying the horrific death his mind had played out so many times in his mind. His fear froze him and he sank to the bottom, paralysed.

Abruptly, his body ripped upwards and burst through the surface. He flailed and splashed with his eyes rolled back in his head, still suffocating.

'Aaron!'

Reggie dragged him from the tub, and Aaron dropped to his knees, vomiting a jet of water and bile onto the ground.

'Breathe!'

He coughed and spat, hunched up in a ball, shaking more from terror than the cold. Reggie knelt beside him and patted his back.

'Are you okay?' Reggie asked.

Aaron did not answer. He stood weakly, his body trembling. Reggie wrapped the robe around him and led him back inside. He sat down heavily on a kitchen chair. Reggie hurried through the darkened house to the living room and returned with a blanket. When she flicked the kitchen light switch, nothing happened.

'Shoot. The storm knocked out the electricity.' She set the blanket on Aaron's lap. 'Talk to me.'

'I'll live.' He wrapped the blanket around himself. 'But I'm never going to be a deep-sea diver, no matter what they tell me on Career Day.'

Reggie dug out a flashlight from one of the kitchen drawers

while Aaron went to put on dry clothes. When he came back, his backpack was slung over his shoulder, and the colour had returned to his face.

'So. Did I make it?' he asked.

Reggie avoided his eyes.

'That's really not important –'

'Come on, how long? So I didn't make a full minute. Fifty-five seconds? Fifty?'

'Aaron, I –'

'For crying out loud, Reg.' Aaron grabbed the stopwatch from her before she could stop him. He peered at the numbers on the display: *0:19*.

'Nineteen seconds? That's it?' Aaron cried. 'That's pathetic!'

'At least you're not a Vour.'

'No, still pussy-boy Aaron.'

'Aaron, it's not a big deal. Just a stupid game.'

'I need to go.'

Reggie didn't want to make it worse for him. 'Okay. Call me tomorrow?'

'Sure.' Aaron strode out of the front door, and it banged shut behind him.

As soon as he was gone, Reggie clicked on the flashlight and headed upstairs. The hallway was much colder than downstairs, and as she passed Henry's room she felt a cold draught underneath his door. *Squeak – squeak – squeak* went the hamster wheel inside. She opened the door and approached Henry's bed. He slept peacefully.

'He's got to be freezing.' Reggie pulled a wool blanket from the foot of the bed.

She shivered and looked around – it felt like someone else was in the room. A sweep of the flashlight's beam illuminated little toy racecars scattered on the floor and snowboarder posters tacked to the walls. Kappy the Koala stared blankly from his perch on the toy box. On the nightstand sat the picture of the family at the Bottle Hill fairgrounds. Reggie picked it up. It was one of the last photos taken of the four of them before Mom had left. Now it was just her and Henry and General Squeak.

She put the picture back and flashed the light across the window. The glass was cracked. Jagged silvery lines spread across it like a spider's web.

'Everything's falling apart around here,' she muttered.

Reggie glanced at Henry once more before she headed down the dark hallway, shivering.

4

The Halloway house was like many in Cutter's Wedge: an old Victorian, three storeys high, with sharply pointed gables. Thick shutters fended off the pugnacious New England winds. The kitchen was its heart, the place where the family could meet for more than two or three minutes at a time in the semi-ordered chaos that was modern life.

But since the day Mom had left without a word, without even saying goodbye, it was the kitchen where her absence was most painfully felt.

Reggie set plates in front of her father and an empty chair, then called, 'Henry! Come on!'

Thom Halloway stared at a construction blueprint in front of him, tapping his coffee mug with his long fingers. Reggie had always loved his fingers – strong and crooked from hammering a million nails into wood and plasterboard. While he was building their back deck when she was seven, he'd taught her how to wield a hammer and saw. 'You want something done, do it yourself,' he'd said. That was his creed. Not that he felt there was anything partic-ularly noble about being self-sufficient. It just meant you'd have to deal with fewer people, which to his way of thinking was always a

31

good thing. The fact that over the years Thom Halloway had moved up from carpenter to contractor held more than a little irony. As he himself admitted, Dad was 'interpersonally challenged'.

'Henry, it's getting cold!'

Footsteps clunked down the stairs – and then tumbled.

'Henry?' called Dad. 'You okay?'

'Yeah!'

Henry walked in, rubbing his elbow.

'I tripped.' He sat down and rubbed his hands together. 'Somebody turn up the heat.'

Reggie glanced at her brother. He looked pasty, with grey circles round his eyes.

'Are you feeling all right?'

'Uh-huh.' Henry frowned at the runny yellow goop on the plate in front of him. He poked it with his fork.

'What is this stuff?'

'Eggs,' said Reggie.

'They're all . . . *wet*.'

'The other day you said they were too *hard*, so I –'

'Well, I didn't mean to make them gross.' Henry pushed his plate away. 'I want cereal.'

Henry stood and bumped the table, splashing his father's coffee onto the blueprint. Dad jumped up.

'Damn it!' he yelled. He swiped at the blueprints with his hands while Reggie hurried over with some paper towels.

'You cursed. Mom says not to curse,' Henry said.

Reggie stopped sopping up the coffee and looked at him. Henry stared at the mess without expression; there was no guilt or concern in his eyes.

'Your mom said a lot of things, Henry.' Dad's hands shook as he scooped up his papers. 'But she's gone now.'

His cell phone rang. Her father's large, rough hand pushed a tiny button and held the thin, dainty device to his ear.

'Halloway.' He listened for a moment, and then huffed. 'I told the crew not to lay the rebar until – damn it –'

'Curse,' Henry mumbled.

'Don't pull it up until I get there. Thirty minutes.' He slapped the phone shut and started out of the kitchen.

'Dad, you didn't eat,' said Reggie.

'I'll grab something on the way to work.' He threw on his coat and headed for the door. 'I'll be home late. Don't wait up.'

Reggie sighed and sat back down.

'So much for a nice family breakfast.'

'I didn't mean to spill the coffee,' Henry said as he poured himself a heaping bowl of Frosted Stars.

'It wasn't the coffee.' Reggie tried not to get upset, but having no place to aim her anger just made it harder. 'Why did you have to bring up Mom, Henry? You know how he gets.'

'Yeah, I know. Sorry.'

Reggie peered at him. Though the words sounded like a quasi-apology, his voice was harsh, remorseless. But he looked totally normal. She pushed away her plate of now-cold eggs.

Henry slid the sugar bowl over and plunged his spoon into it. He added a heaping white mound to his pre-sugared cereal. Then another, and then another. Reggie looked on, her eyebrows rising.

'Do you want some cereal with your sugar?' she asked.

'I like it this way,' said Henry as he dumped one more big spoonful and started shovelling the cereal in.

33

'Since when?' asked Reggie.

Henry's spoon stopped halfway to his lips.

'Since *now*.'

They sat there mutely, the only sound the crunch of Henry's chewing. His face was as white as the milk in his bowl. As he ate, he shivered. Reggie reached out and put her palm to his forehead. It was like pressing against a window on a wintry day. Henry recoiled.

'Get off!' he yelled, jumping to his feet and knocking into the table. Cereal sloshed out of the bowl.

'You're ice-cold,' Reggie said, standing up. 'Stay there.'

She walked out. Henry put his own hand against his head, knitted his brow and then shrugged when Reggie came back in with a digital thermometer.

'Open up.'

Henry scowled at the command.

'No.'

'No? Want me to shove this somewhere else?'

Henry's scowl hardened, but he opened his mouth and Reggie put the thermometer in and pushed his jaw closed.

'Now keep your mouth shut. It isn't done till it beeps.'

It took all of two seconds. Reggie took the thermometer out and eyed the readout, frowning.

'Twenty-three point five? Great. It's broken . . . or you're from another planet.'

He stood up and turned his back to her. 'I'm going upstairs.'

For Reggie, the shower had always been a sanctuary. All her senses felt different here. The close, shining walls surrounding her. The steam blurring everything beyond the tile and glass. The pounding water insulating her from all other sound. And lately the sound barrier served a new purpose. It allowed her to give in to her sadness and her anger, to cry about Mom where no one could hear.

Reggie stepped out of the shower, wiped the mirror above the sink clean and stared at herself, sweeping her hair up this way and that, wondering when the minimal curves of her lean body were going to turn into something noticeable to anyone but herself. Mom used to stand beside her and say, 'Don't worry. I didn't have boobs till I was seventeen.' Aaron called Reggie 'flat-top', and he wasn't talking about her hairstyle.

At least she had the hair going for her: long, dark brown curls, just like her mother's. Every week Reggie would sit in front of the mirror, hair washed and gleaming wet, and Mom would give her a trim. Long after the scissors had been put away, they would still be talking. Plenty of time was spent discussing skin creams, make-up and manicures, but these subjects always meandered into deeper conversations about the challenges of school and the complexities of friendship and of love.

There was one conversation Reggie couldn't stop thinking about. They'd had it six months before Mom left.

Mom had been sitting on the toilet lid painting her toenails, and Reggie had asked, 'Mom, do you believe in soul mates?'

'Soul mates? Why?' Mom said.

'I was reading this magazine article in the dentist's office, "How to Find Your Soulmate", or something like that.'

'So do I believe there are people who are "meant to be together"? Is that what you mean?'

'Uh-huh.'

'Boy, I haven't thought about *that* one in a long time.' Mom's faint smile appeared. She wore the same smile whether she was happy or melancholy, so it had been hard to tell what she'd been feeling. 'I guess maybe I still do.'

Reggie remembered the word 'still'.

'The trouble is, Reg, there are billions of people out there, so unless you luck out right away you have a tough choice: either be prepared to spend a good chunk of your life trying to find him, with no guarantees you will – or settle for someone, well, less than a "soul mate".'

Reggie remembered the word 'settle'.

'I guess the first choice takes a lot of guts,' she said.

Mom stared at her, then went back to work on her toes.

These days, Reggie wondered if her simple question had made her mother begin to confront feelings she had buried. Reggie still didn't know if she believed in soul mates, but, if they were out there, the truth was she hoped Mom never found hers.

Reggie put on her robe and pulled it snug around her; school was over for the holiday break, but she had to get ready for work. As she headed back to her room, she heard a voice coming through Henry's door. That was odd. He never shut his door. She put an ear to it. Henry was talking to someone.

'Did that hurt?'

He giggled, but it sounded cruel and cold. He repeated the question.

'Did *that* hurt?'

Reggie slowly turned the knob, opening the door a crack. Henry was sitting on his bed with his back to her.

'What are you doing, Henry?'

Henry froze, then turned towards her, and Reggie caught her breath. In his hands was Kappy, his beloved koala. Chunks of its fur had been torn out, leaving ragged, bald spots. It looked like a torture victim.

'Henry . . . *what are you doing?*'

Henry smiled.

'Seeing what he looks like with no hair. You know . . . naked.'

'But he's your favourite.'

'It doesn't *hurt*, Reg.' He grabbed a clump of the koala's fur and yanked it out. Reggie flinched.

'But why would you –'

'Because it's *mine.*'

Reggie cocked her head. There it was again – his voice. It was raspy and low. Not the voice of an eight-year-old.

'Sure he's yours,' she said, sitting down on the bed next to Henry, 'but that doesn't mean –' She tried to feel his forehead again, but Henry pushed her hand away.

'I feel fine.'

Reggie nodded and took the mangled koala.

'You and Mom won this together at that carnival, remember?'

'I remember.'

'Is that why you want to . . . take Kappy apart? Because it reminds you of Mom?'

'Why would that bother me?' asked Henry. 'Mom's not ever coming back.'

Reggie was surprised by his frankness.

'Henry, yes, she is. Mom is coming back. It's okay to be mad at her – I mean, I'm mad too. But she loves us. She loves you. She needs time, that's all.'

'You can tell yourself that if you want.' Henry looked up at Reggie. 'But it's a lie.'

Reggie gaped at Henry. It had been months since Mom's last e-mail, longer than that since a phone call. Reggie and her father had not wanted to move on yet. Henry, on the other hand . . .

'Are you sure you're feeling okay?' Reggie handed Kappy back to Henry.

He nodded though, despite his flannel pyjamas, his robe and a blanket wrapped around his shoulders, he still shivered.

'I'm late for work,' said Reggie. 'Mrs Boswell will be here in a few minutes, once she gets out of church. But maybe I should call Eben and tell him I can't make it . . .'

'Jeez, Reggie, I'm fine!'

'Okay, okay. But today you need to stay warm and dry. I'll leave a note for Mrs B to make you some soup. Now, I know she can get a bit cranky, but she's the only babysitter we could –'

'I'm not a baby, Reggie.'

'I know. Sometimes it feels like you're older than I am.' She kissed his cheek. It was cold.

'Close the door, okay?'

As she closed the door behind her, Reggie heard Henry whispering to himself again.

5

Small as it was, a person could live in Cutter's Wedge and find almost everything they'd need there, especially if they liked to read. There was a well-stocked library and four bookstores, including Reggie's favourite, Something Wicked. Eben Bloch had moved into town two years ago to open it.

Something Wicked seemed to materialize as a safe haven for Reggie in the year before Mom left, when things between her parents were strained at best and explosive at worst. Mom's behaviour became increasingly strange and secretive; Dad's turned angry and suspicious. It came to an ugly head one night when Dad confronted Mom about the password lock on her laptop. Reggie couldn't stomach it any more and fled to the bookstore for shelter.

Amid the dusty shelves she had spotted a well-thumbed copy of Edgar Gordon's classic *Night-Gaunt* and shelled out ten dollars for the book. Anything to keep her mind off the storms at home. The silver-haired man behind the counter had looked fondly at her purchase before handing it back over to her, saying, 'Good choice. Do you read much horror?'

Since then, she'd worked there Wednesdays and Thursdays for two hours after school, and Saturdays from ten until five.

The bookstore had once been a tavern with a high, pressed tin ceiling and a few apartments above. Its jovial proprietor had been as famous for his wife running out on him as he'd been for his whiskey sours. Years after she'd vanished, when an upstairs boarder noticed some loose plaster in the bathroom and decided to fix it himself, he discovered that the notorious lady hadn't run off anywhere. She'd been wrapped neatly from ankles to lips in duct tape, hung on a meat hook and boarded up behind a shower wall. Eben swore that sometimes, late at night, he heard her ghost groaning.

That bit of history suited Something Wicked perfectly. Eben stocked a solid selection of classics and bestsellers, but Something Wicked focused on all things gothic, gruesome and grisly. There were tilting stacks of books everywhere and no apparent sense of order or classification in the racks, though Eben always knew where everything was. The lights he installed in the tin ceiling spread grey shadows throughout the place, so even sunny days offered dozens of dim and private places to sit and read.

Eben was up on a footstool stacking books when Reggie entered. As always, he wore a suit, which was funny since some days not a single person walked into the store; Eben made most of his sales through his website. Reggie had never seen him without his pocket handkerchief, much less in jeans. His hair was silver, and he wore small, wire-rimmed glasses that he sometimes blamed for his headaches.

'You're late,' he said, not turning round.

'You're old,' she replied, stashing her stuff behind the counter.

Eben grinned.

'Reggie, you have no idea *how* old.' He was precise yet not stuffy in conversation. His accent defied classification, lilting on some words, throaty on others. Eben claimed to be from too many places to name – none of them interesting. He stepped down with his habitual grunt, grabbed his steel-tipped cane and limped towards her. Reggie wasn't sure how he'd got the injury; she assumed it was in a war because she knew he'd once been a soldier, but he never talked about it. He raised his cane and pointed at a half-finished book display in a corner.

'That was supposed to be done *yesterday*. Finish it, please.'

'Yes, sir, right away,' Reggie said. 'We sure want to be ready for the horde of last-minute Christmas shoppers.'

Eben lowered his glasses down his nose at her, which meant his patience was wearing thin. She got the message and went to work, constructing a 'house of books' on the table with hardcover copies of Stephen King's latest, and Eben settled into a leather wingback chair.

'Pick your poison,' he said. 'Poe or Lovecraft?'

Reggie grinned at the start of their ritual.

'Mmm . . . Poe,' she said.

'All right.' Eben thought for a moment. '"Masque of the Red Death". First line.'

'Maybe we should play patty cake,' said Reggie. 'How about a challenge?'

'Let's hear it, Miss Halloway,' he said.

'Okay,' she said, closing her eyes. '"The Red Death had long devastated the country. No pestilence had ever been so fatal, or so hideous. Blood was its Avatar and its seal – the redness and horror of blood."' She opened her eyes. Eben was smiling.

'Almost perfect,' he said. 'You left out a "the" but we'll give it to you.'

Reggie resumed balancing the novels one on top of the other.

'My turn,' she said. 'Poe or Lovecraft?'

'Lovecraft,' said Eben.

'Okay,' she said. '"The Rats in the Walls". Last sentence.'

'A nice choice,' Eben said. He cocked his head in thought, and then spoke in a hushed tone. '"The slithering scurrying rats whose scampering will never let me sleep; the demon rats that race behind the padding in this room and beckon me down to greater horrors than I have ever known; the rats they can never hear; the rats, the rats in the walls."'

'Sounds good to me,' said Reggie, fitting one more book in at an angle. The house collapsed. She sighed. 'Typical of this stupid day.'

'What's the matter?'

'Oh, Henry's sick and being weird.'

'Weird?'

'He pulled all the fur off his favourite stuffed animal. He said he wanted to see what it looked like naked. Weird enough?'

'Does your dad know?'

'He wasn't home.'

'You should tell him.'

'Why? He won't do anything. It works for him because he doesn't *notice* anything, either.'

Reggie sat on a stool opposite Eben.

'Your father loves you, Regina,' he said. 'He's learning to cope with a big change. Give him a chance.'

'And *I* know how to cope? I just started high school! And now I've got a mothering gig to boot.'

'Unforeseen challenges. You do the best you can. Henry will be okay.'

'Henry doesn't have his mom any more.'

'But he has you.'

Reggie smiled a little. This was why she loved her conversations with Eben. He didn't sugarcoat, he didn't make excuses and he didn't treat her like a snotty teenager. He was everything her father wasn't.

'And I've got you,' she said.

'Yes, you do.' Eben smiled back. 'Always. Poor girl.'

The bell on the door jingled and Aaron walked in wearing his pith helmet.

'My book come in, Eben?'

'That it did, my lad.' Eben pulled a parcel from behind the counter. Aaron ripped off the brown paper wrapping.

'What is it?' asked Reggie.

'*Murder, Mayhem and Madness: A History of Serial Killers!*'

Reggie rolled her eyes. 'Not more serial killers.'

'This is great stuff, Reg,' said Aaron, flipping through the book. 'Take Richard Chase, the "Vampire of Sacramento". He put the blood and brains of his victims in a blender and then drank them; he thought his blood was turning to powder and he needed fresh goods to replenish it.'

Reggie grimaced. 'Thanks for sharing.'

'You like your horror to stay make-believe,' Aaron said. 'I like mine served up real.'

'So was last night real or make-believe?' asked Reggie.

'What happened last night?' asked Eben.

Aaron grinned.

'Oh, last night we did a fear –' He caught Reggie's warning eye.

'Fear *what*?' Eben asked.

'Nothing. Just a dumb game,' said Reggie. 'You know – geek stuff.'

Eben looked her over.

'Don't ever go into politics, Regina,' he said. 'You can't lie to save your life. What did you two do last night?'

Reggie knew that tone. You could tell Eben *anything* and never worry about being judged, but he was not a person you lied to.

'We, uh, took a fear test. A ritual, sort of.'

'I failed,' Aaron confessed. 'Not exactly the apt pupil. But Reggie passed with flying colours.'

'Ritual?' Eben asked. 'What ritual?'

Reggie sighed, pulled the journal from her backpack and then handed it to Eben. He adjusted his glasses, opened the book and read the first paragraph aloud:

The Vours are all around us. They wear our names and faces, but they are not us. The most dangerous thing we are ever told is, 'There is nothing to be afraid of,' because, in truth, there is so very much to fear.

Eben glanced from Reggie to Aaron.

'Where did you get this?' he asked.

44

'It came in with one of the shipments. A few weeks ago,' Reggie answered, doing her best to sound nonchalant. 'No idea who wrote it.'

Eben flipped through the pages, scanning the spidery handwriting. Here and there he stopped to examine a sketch or a diagram.

'I don't mind if you borrow books, but I expect you to tell me when you do,' he said. 'And it would be nice if I could at least see it myself first. This is a singular find, Regina.'

'It's just the diary of some crazy old kook, Eben. She writes about these monsters called the Vours that attack humans when they're most afraid – like, can't-speak-or-blink-or-breathe afraid. They take over your body and send your consciousness to some demonic hell, then they live your life out. And they look and act like regular humans, so it's impossible to tell who's a Vour and who's not. A pretty fun read, actually.'

'Better than most trashy thriller novels, I'd say,' added Aaron.

Eben stopped at another page.

'*On the Winter Solstice night, shun your fears. Bury them. I know it. I saw it. They'll take your soul.*' Eben looked up and scowled. 'The winter solstice was last night. And you tempted these creatures to come take you?'

'Eben,' Reggie said, 'we were just playing around.'

'No,' said Eben. 'Cowboys and Indians is playing around.'

'Don't tell Native Americans that,' Reggie said.

'Come on, Eben,' said Aaron. 'It's not real.'

Eben closed the book.

'Aaron. Reggie. Nobody loves settling down with a horror tale and getting chilled to the bone more than I.' He waved a hand around the store. 'It's my life! But *this* . . .' He rapped the book with his knuckles. 'This is insanity. This is *cult*. Dark magic, chants, rituals, secrets . . .'

'All that stuff is our bread and butter!' Reggie countered.

'Yes, but we sell fiction. You don't know anything about this book, or where it came from.'

'We know it's not real,' Reggie said.

'But ritualizing makes something real *in here*.' He tapped his head. 'And that's when it gets dangerous. So, the author . . .' He wagged the book at Reggie. 'Ever wondered what happened to *her*?'

Reggie and Aaron shrugged.

'It's just a book –'

'A book that doesn't belong to you.'

'I'm sorry, Eben,' said Reggie, 'I won't do it again. But it's not like we believe in it.'

'If you didn't believe in the possibility, you wouldn't have challenged these creatures. And the minute you start to believe in something, it begins to have power over you.'

The door jingled and two black-clad goth girls from Cutter High slinked in.

'Customers, Regina.' Eben turned to greet the girls. 'Go finish the display. I feel a holiday rush coming on.'

———

A little after five, Reggie waved goodbye to Eben and headed home. It was already dark.

The ice reflected green and red from the Christmas lights

strung across lampposts. Cutter's Wedge Wines had its annual window display of gnomes toasting each other with rosy-cheeked grins. Safko's Hardware had its plump styrofoam snowman out on the sidewalk, spade in hand. Mr Safko had given it glass eyes instead of using coal or black buttons, and the effect was more unsettling than festive. The eyes were too realistic. They gave the impression that a living human was trapped inside the snowman, his wide eyes pleading for rescue, his mouth unable to scream.

Reggie paused under the lamppost where her bicycle was locked. She was bothered by Eben's reaction to her having taken *The Devouring*, and even more troubled by his attitude about what she and Aaron had done with it. It was certainly possible that whoever had written it was completely mad – where there wasn't scrawling handwriting, the author had sketched horrible images of smoky monsters, people with their eyes scratched out and cryptic symbols. But insanity, as far as she knew, wasn't contagious.

A sharp hiss startled Reggie, and she looked up. Steam rose from a manhole cover across the street. A sudden gust sent the vapours whirling, and for a moment two figures were revealed behind, one much smaller than the other, huddled together, talking.

Reggie's pulse stuttered. She squinted, but the wind died and the steam folded back on itself like a curtain. She got up. She thought she knew the smaller person.

Reggie crossed the street towards them, when a white light burst out of the night. She raised an arm to shield her eyes, and looked into the headlights of an oncoming truck. She froze for an instant, watching the driver's face, hearing the angry horn and screeching brakes. She darted out of the way just as the truck sped past. The two figures turned at the commotion.

'Henry!' cried Reggie, racing up to him. 'What are you doing here?'

'Just, you know, coming to see you,' Henry said with a shrug. 'Mrs Boswell fell asleep.'

'Do you know what Dad would do if he knew you were out after dark?'

'That's what I was just telling him.'

Reggie's attention shifted to the other figure. She recognized the sweet smell instantly.

'Is this your little brother?' Quinn asked. He popped his gum and smiled.

Reggie nodded. 'My soon-to-be-*murdered* little brother.'

'I was giving him the "Don't walk around by yourself after dark" lecture.' Quinn hesitated. 'God, I sound like my mom.'

'I know the feeling,' said Reggie.

'It was light out when I started,' Henry said.

'So what brings you onto these evil streets after sunset?' Reggie asked nervously.

Quinn took his backpack off his shoulder. 'Funny you should ask. You work at that bookstore, right?'

'Uh-huh.' Reggie was unable to form sentences again.

'I have something for you.'

He pulled a book out of the pack and handed it to Reggie. If it was even possible for Quinn to look sheepish, he did now.

'A thank-you for bailing me out the other day. You saved my butt in English class.'

Reggie looked at the cover; it was an ornate, leather-bound edition of Bram Stoker's *Dracula*.

'I confess,' said Quinn, 'I'm a closet horror buff. We can be geeks together.'

Reggie blushed. 'I don't know what to say.'

'Just say we'll hang out some time, okay?'

'Of course.' Reggie beamed. Henry looked from his sister to Quinn and rolled his eyes.

'Can we go already?' he demanded.

Quinn looked down at Henry. 'No more walking around at night, right? There are worse things than vampires out here.' He winked at Reggie and walked away. Reggie stood dumbfounded for a few more seconds, then turned to her brother.

'You were supposed to stay put. You're sick.'

'I feel fine.'

'So what else did you talk about with Quinn?'

'Not you, if that's what you're asking.'

'I wasn't – come on. We're going home.'

Henry walked silently beside her as she pushed her bike along the roadside. It wasn't just Mrs Boswell being such an incompetent guardian, or Henry sneaking out in the dead of winter, that pissed her off so much. The truth was, she didn't want to be the 'Mommy'. She didn't want to make dinner and do the laundry and the vacuuming. She didn't want to have to look after Henry, *and* take his temperature, *and* worry about him, *and* scold him. She wanted Mom, wherever she was, to stop being a selfish jerk and come home.

When they got back to the house, Dad's truck was still gone: a stroke of luck for everyone. Henry bounded up the stairs to his bedroom without a word, not even giving Reggie a chance to send him there. She kicked off her soggy wet sneakers and stormed into the living room.

'Mrs Boswell!'

The old woman was slumped on the couch, her hair a silvery mop. The DVD menu cycled endlessly, playing the same forty-five-second clip of music over and over again. An untouched cup of tea sat on the table before her.

'Mrs Boswell?'

Reggie crept closer, reaching out to take the woman's shoulder and gently shake her. The old lady's head flopped to the side, her hair tumbled from her face, and her blank, unblinking eyes stared into Reggie's own. Her face had contorted into a rictus of terror. She was dead.

6

Reggie's dad came home just in time to see Mrs Boswell being wheeled out of the house on a stretcher.

The ambulance rolled away without even turning on its lights or sirens. The babysitter had been pronounced dead on site by the coroner – a heart attack, most likely. Henry had watched them take the body away, then shut himself in his room. Once the dust had settled, Dad poured himself a scotch, sat down at the kitchen table and stared out into the winter night. Reggie stood in the doorway, watching him.

'Dad?'

He took a sip of his drink. 'Yes, hon?'

'What should we tell Henry?'

'I don't know.' He was quiet for a moment. 'She was old. People die. He's only eight, but I'm pretty sure he knows that.'

'Yeah.' Reggie frowned. 'That's a big help, Dad.'

She walked briskly out of the kitchen, leaving her father to drink alone. The glow of their sad little Christmas tree left the living room steeped in shadow. Dad had brought it home the week before, and that evening had been a happy one, rare in their house these days. They'd dragged out the box of ornaments from the closet, smiling and laughing. Dad had belted out Christmas carols in his booming voice as they unpacked them; Reggie had thought he was laying it on a bit thick, but with Mom missing she couldn't blame him for trying. Henry had run around the tree tossing fistfuls of tinsel at it, and the family spent the whole evening piling on the shiny orbs and angels and garlands, as if covering up the tree's bare spots would cover up the gaping hole that was Mom's absence.

Tonight, in the multicoloured gloom of the tree's lights, Reggie thought again of her mother. She pictured her decorating someone else's tree. She wondered if she were happy, or if she missed her family. She wondered if she were dead. Dead like Mrs Boswell. Dead and gone.

The old woman's cold cup of tea still sat on the coffee table. Reggie stared at it for a long time, then picked it up, tossed the tea in the sink and put the mug in the dishwasher. She went upstairs to her bedroom.

Reggie couldn't sleep. Whenever she closed her eyes, the image of the dead woman's face rose from the dark. Her mind raced. Why was Henry acting so strangely? And what had he really been doing walking around by himself? She had tried to bring it up again on their walk home, but Henry had just kicked a stick down the sidewalk, refusing to say a word. Reggie had marched along, as angry as she was relieved, and thanking God that Quinn had bumped into her little brother.

She smiled in the dark. Quinn.

There was a person she'd never expected would enter her realm of existence. Nothing made Reggie Halloway's palms sweat, not even her first viewing of *Psycho* – but Quinn did. Was he really interested in her? He wasn't the big-headed jock she'd expected. He was smart, sweet and a horror freak to boot. What parallel universe had she entered?

Reggie twisted again in her bed, smacked her fist into the pillow and tried to find a comfortable spot for her spinning head.

Henry.

He was mixed up, deeply troubled, doing battle with his own demons – and she didn't know how to help him. Horror wasn't something terrible she witnessed on a movie screen or read in a book any more. It was real. It surrounded her, and nobody would face it until it was too late.

Dad still acted like Mom was on some long business trip. Like she'd come through the front door any day now, tanned, tired, but happy to be home, arms full of lame T-shirts and gift-shop snow globes, eyes full of love for him, for her and for Henry . . .

Without realizing it, Reggie had pushed away her covers and sat up in bed, her knees pulled to her chest. She heard something . . . music . . .

'*You better watch out, you better not cry . . .*'

Reggie looked at the clock. The red digital numbers glowed 12:41. Either some carollers were pulling an all-nighter or Dad was still awake with his scotch and playing the goofy Christmas album Mom loved.

'*You better not pout, I'm telling you why . . .*'

Reggie got out of bed, shivering as the cold air hugged her body. She grabbed her robe and went out into the hall.

'*Santa Claus is coming to town.*'

The wooden steps felt like marble beneath her bare feet. It was colder downstairs.

'*He's making a list, he's checking it twice . . .*'

The voices were coming from the front yard.

'*He's gonna find out who's naughty or nice . . .*'

Reggie pulled her robe snug and walked into the living room. It was dark except for the tree's blinking lights. Dad was standing at the square picture window, holding Henry in his arms.

'Dad, what's going on?'

Reggie came up beside them. Outside, five children sang, their carolling books obscuring their faces. White breath wafted from behind the books and snaked into the darkness. A light snow was falling, sticking to their coats and hats and scarves, sparkling in the glow of the porch lamp like magic dust. Henry yawned.

'*Santa Claus is coming to town.*'

Reggie shivered and moved closer to her father.

'It's almost one o'clock in the morning,' she said. 'What are they doing here?'

'*We see you when you're sleeping . . .*'

Reggie reached for her father's hand.

'*We know when you're awake . . .*'

'Daddy,' said Henry, 'I don't like them.'

'I knew they'd come.' Dad bowed his head. 'I'm so sorry, Regina.'

The children's voices turned raspy.

'*We know if you've been bad or good . . .*'

The carollers lowered their books.

They were children, but not human – red and green veins

54

criss-crossed their ashen skin, and their sunken eyes peered out, red as blood. Henry buried his head in his father's chest.

The smallest of them stepped forward and smiled; its fangs flashed like polished daggers.

'*We're with you,*' it hissed. '*We'll always be with you.*'

'Daddy!' Reggie wailed.

With an ungodly screech, the demons crashed through the window, taloned hands outstretched, and knocked Reggie into the Christmas tree. The tree toppled, ornaments bursting into a thousand gleaming pieces. The shards ripped into her flesh, and blood poured from dozens of tiny wounds in her arms, neck and cheeks. All around her, the brightly wrapped presents split open like living organs, spilling out fetid, rusty-red ooze.

Dad didn't fight the demons as they ripped Henry from his arms; he simply dropped to his knees and hung his head.

'Don't let them get me!' Henry screamed. 'Reggie, help!'

Reggie stumbled to her knees.

'Daddy!' she cried. 'Help him! Save him!'

Blood dripped down her forehead as she lurched for Henry, but the wiry branches of the Christmas tree wrapped round her wrists and ankles like chains and yanked her backwards.

The creatures turned on her. Saliva dripped from their fangs as they approached. Fear, like death's icy grip, froze her in place. One of the demons smiled and brushed her bloody cheek with a long, grotesque finger.

'You're weak, scared. You're a cripple,' it hissed. 'You're *all* cripples.'

The spot where the demon's finger had touched Reggie's face

ached with a sharp and wicked cold. She felt the blood congeal on her skin. Flesh cracked like thin ice. She looked down in horror as puzzle-sized pieces of her fell to the floor and splintered. In moments her face was no more than a white skull.

'Reggie!' Henry cried.

Amid his screams, Reggie heard faint music – a calliope tune that sounded familiar. The demon children chanted as they dragged Henry out of the broken picture window.

Once he's gone, there's no way back.
Once he's in, there's no way out.
Left to linger in the black,
Lost to endless fear and doubt . . .

Henry's fading cry mingled with the horrible chorus.

'No way out . . . no way out . . . no way out . . .'

Reggie shot up in bed. The terror swelled in her windpipe. The air couldn't get past it to her lungs.

Gradually, her ragged gasps slowed. She leaped out of bed – she had to make sure that Henry was okay.

Reggie tiptoed across the hall and peeked into Henry's room. General Squeak screeched at the sudden intrusion and scampered around in the dark.

'Henry?' Reggie called. 'Henry, wake up!'

She flicked on the light. The quilt was askew, the hapless, mauled Kappy lay sprawled on the floor, but Henry was gone. She ransacked the sheets of the empty bed and swung open the closet door. Nothing. She ran down the hall to the bathroom, turned the light on and pulled back the shower curtain. Nothing. The guest room. Nothing. Back towards Dad's room.

Where was he? Was she still dreaming? Had he been scared by the dark, and gone to sleep by Dad?

She peeked into the master bedroom. Her father snored low and deep. She tiptoed to the far side of the king-size bed and patted the comforter, but Dad was sleeping alone.

Reggie sprinted back into the hall and down the stairs. The smell of smoke poked at her nose.

She paused, and, hearing the crackling of burning wood in the fireplace, headed towards the den. The room was dark but for the amber glow of the fire, which cast Henry's shadow, long and distorted, on the wall. He knelt in front of the fireplace, a checkered afghan draped across his back. Reggie stepped down the two stone stairs into the room. Henry spoke without turning around.

'Needed to warm up, sis. That's all.' His voice was icy calm as he prodded the embers with a poker. 'Dad never fixed the cracks in my window. The cold still gets in.'

Reggie inched forward. Though he spoke softly, his voice sounded . . . *older*.

'You're not supposed to be doing that, Henry. You know what Dad says about messing around with fire.'

'Dad doesn't care. I could burn the whole house down and he wouldn't even get out of bed.'

'Come on.' Reggie squatted beside her brother, tilting her head to view him in profile. Shadows from the fire played on his skin. 'You don't mean that. Dad loves us. He loves you. He's here for us a hundred per cent.'

'Dad's old and lost and afraid. You can smell the fear on him. Like rotting fruit.'

'Why did you leave the house today, Henry? Were you afraid? It's okay. Tell me the truth.'

Henry's arctic blue eyes sparkled.

'No, I wasn't afraid of anything.'

Reggie clutched his arm. Its coldness shocked her.

'Henry, I want to help you. *Talk* to me.'

'I don't need help. I'm fine,' he said simply. He stretched a hand to the fire and waved his fingers above the bright, wagging tongues, smiling like a child with new friends. He stretched his arm further, his hand lower, stroking the flames.

'Henry! No!'

Reggie lunged at him, and they went tumbling away from the fire. Henry dropped the poker and it clanged onto the floor; the tip landed on the oval carpet and the wool smouldered. Reggie looked down at him.

'Are you *nuts*?'

Henry stared at the blaze. The flames flickered in his eyes.

'I just wanted to see how hot it was.'

Henry looked at his hand. It was red, and the tips of his fingers had already blistered. He examined it like a new toy.

'It feels . . . funny.'

'Henry, we've got to run that under cold water. I don't know what is going on in your head lately, but you know what fire –'

Their father stormed into the den.

'What the *hell* is going on?'

He stamped out the rug with his bare foot, leaving a blackened circle the size of a quarter, then picked up the poker and

58

slammed it back into its stand. He grabbed Reggie by the collar, lifted her off Henry, and dropped her on the other side of the hearth.

'Who lit this damned fire?' he hollered.

'Henry did,' said Reggie. 'I was just trying to stop him from burning himself.'

'*Me?*' cried Henry. 'I didn't do it! I don't even know *how* to make a fire! The smoke smell woke me up. She said I'd be sorry if I told on her, and she pushed me at the fire.' He thrust his hand up at Dad. 'See?'

'He's – he's lying!' Reggie stuttered, stunned. 'He started it! I came downstairs because he wasn't in bed! I was worried about him!'

Dad's lips curdled. '*Worried?* You were beating him up!'

'No, I wasn't! I was trying to stop him from hurting himself!'

'Regina!' Dad bellowed. 'There will be no lying in this house. Are we clear?'

He was boiling. But he wasn't the only one.

'You are *so* wrong about this, Dad!'

Dad suddenly swatted the fire screen with his arm and knocked it over. 'I thought I could depend on you, Regina. I thought this family mattered –'

Dad was looking at his daughter but he was seeing some-one else.

'Don't you dare,' she seethed. 'I'm not *her*.'

Dad's anger deflated before Reggie's eyes. He looked at the floor, because he couldn't bear to look at his daughter.

Henry squeezed Dad's leg.

'We know you love us, Dad. You're here for us a hundred per

cent.' Henry peered out at Reggie. A grin flitted across his face. She fumed, but she knew she'd lost.

'Can I go to my room now?' she said.

Dad nodded. Reggie glared at Henry and marched out. She heard Dad behind her.

'And as for you, little man, let's fix up that hand and get you in bed. I'll bring you an extra blanket. You're freezing.'

7

Dad left for work before dawn Christmas Eve morning. He had a new development contract for a subdivision of low-income housing in the poor, ghostly town of Wennemack, a half-hour's drive from Cutter's Wedge. The ground was frozen solid and no foundation work would begin until the end of March, but Reggie's father was a meticulous planner who would take a small crew to new sites months in advance and map out every step a dozen times before spring arrived. He'd promised his crew an early finish so they could go home for Christmas Eve dinner with their families. Reggie wondered if he felt the same obligation to his own family.

From bed Reggie smelled the burned coffee wafting up the stairs. Her dad drank mud-like coffee, black, thick and sugarless, a bitter but familiar aroma that evoked the comfort of predictable routine. That felt like a lifetime ago to Reggie now.

Dad had confined her to the house for the day, and even though he was gone until tonight, she was pretty much under house arrest. He'd call home every hour or so, making sure she picked up. She'd violated the rules once before and it cost her an entire month of cell phone, friends and freedom. Even if she snuck out for an hour and made it back before the next check-in, Henry would snitch for sure.

Henry. He'd turned on her last night.

They'd fought countless times before; argued, yelled, wrestled, argued, slapped, smacked. Henry had tattled, baited, blamed, annoyed, meddled and eavesdropped on her like any little brother. But he'd never lied. Not until last night.

Reggie pulled on a pair of maroon cords and her favourite grey hoodie as she thought through a plan of attack. With Dad gone for the day and just her and Henry in the house, maybe she could get through to him. She'd make Henry's favourite breakfast, chocolate-chip waffles, and then they could get down to it and really talk. Tomorrow was their first Christmas without Mom, and Reggie knew that was at the core of all this. How couldn't it be?

Reggie headed for the bathroom to pee and wash her face, but stopped in the hallway. It was still and cold. Something felt different.

She walked towards Henry's room. The door was open, and she realized why the silence bothered her; there was no incessant scritching of tiny claws on glass, no high-pitched twittering or rusty cheeps from that obnoxious spinning wheel. Dawn to late morning was General Squeak's most active time, when he would run and skitter and scratch about until he curled up and fell asleep around noon. But not this morning.

Reggie pushed the door open and peeked in. Henry was still asleep, his brown curls spread across his pillow. He had a heavy wool blanket over his thick down comforter, even though Dad had cranked up the heat that morning. Henry had to be swelter-ing, but his covers rose and fell in perfect calm.

The floor of the hamster cage was littered with pine shavings and gnawed corncobs. Clear plastic tubes of various colours and widths sprawled into terrarium compartments that each housed some silly piece of rodent furniture: a truck, a lounge chair and a play tunnel.

Reggie tiptoed to the cage and looked for General Squeak, but the hamster was nowhere to be found. The wheel on the bottom level was on its side, and the small water dish was knocked over. The door latch was unlocked.

Henry occasionally left the cage open by mistake, and his inquisitive pet had escaped a few times before. His favourite destination was the bathroom at the end of the hall, and once there he took whatever delight hamsters take in chewing on empty toilet paper rolls, snotty tissues and used dental floss. The last time Reggie found the fugitive hamster, he had squirmed into the bathroom cabinet and gnawed through a box of her tampons.

She crept back out of Henry's room and headed for the bathroom, half expecting to find him up on the sink, where he would have left a lovely pile of hamster turds on Dad's shaving kit.

No such bad luck; the bathroom was vacant. But the toilet gurgled and choked at her.

'Damn it, I thought Dad was going to fix this,' Reggie muttered. She jiggled the handle and flushed. The water level swelled. Up and up it swirled, threatening to rise above the porcelain rim.

'You've got to be kidding me.' She grabbed the plunger and shoved it in. 'Merry Christmas Eve, Reggie!'

The drain opened and sucked in a huge glop of water. The toilet chugged a couple of times but then stopped, the returning water unable to rise more than a few centimetres above the hole. Reggie cursed silently as the shallow water rippled. Then a small, leathery strip slid into view beneath the water's surface. At first Reggie mistook it for a clump of hair. She looked closer and slapped her hand over her mouth.

A tail.

Reggie found rubber gloves under the sink and snapped them on. Now she could see that a hind leg had emerged from the hole. '*Oh, no . . .*'

She plunged her hand in and grabbed the hamster's slimy leg. Reggie felt the tiniest crack of bone within the already mangled limb. She pulled. Ribs poked through the skin like broken toothpicks.

The hamster was practically shapeless, little more than a drenched pile of hair and flesh. Reggie stood and stroked the hamster's fur.

For two years she had watched Henry nurture the annoying ball of squeaks and peeps, had watched him roll across the living room floor in his stupid plastic ball, had come to see the dumb thing whenever he climbed inside a plastic television Henry had bought with his birthday money.

'Look, Reggie!' Henry would giggle. 'It's the General Squeak Show!'

How do I tell him? Reggie asked herself.

The ringing phone made her start, and General Squeak's broken body slipped from her hand and dropped to the floor with a splat. She heard Henry scamper into her father's bedroom, where he answered the phone. Reggie picked up the crushed hamster, pumped two foamy dollops of scented soap onto the rodent's body, and ran it under the faucet.

'Reggie!' Henry hollered from the hall. 'It's Dad! He wants to talk to you!'

'Tell him I'll call him back!'

Reggie cringed as the soap foamed over the hamster's dead, open eyes. Strange, she thought, how when the essence of even the smallest living thing vanishes, the world feels colder and bigger. She wiped his black eyes with her pinky.

'Now, he said! He wants to know you're in the house 'cause you're grounded!'

'God, Henry! I'm in the bathroom!'

She shut the water off and blotted General Squeak with a facecloth. She wrapped the little corpse with it and stood in the middle of the tiled floor, unsure what to do next. Henry's footsteps came closer.

'What are you doing in there?'

'Parasailing, Henry!' she shouted angrily, kicking the door completely shut. 'What do you think I'm doing in here?'

'General Squeak got out of his cage. Have you seen him?'

'No.' It stunned her that her first impulse was to lie. She heard Henry start back towards his room. 'Henry, wait.'

She opened the bathroom door and stepped out, cradling the wrapped towel to her chest. Henry stood in his oversized flannel pyjamas, looking every bit like the boy she knew and loved.

'What? What am I waiting for?'

'Something happened to the General. Something bad.' Reggie unwrapped the outer flap of the towel. 'I think he's dead, Henry.'

'Like Mrs Boswell?'

Reggie chilled. He hadn't mentioned the babysitter since they'd found her body. She had naively hoped that he'd somehow forgotten the ambulance pulling up, the black-jacketed coroner's knock on the door, the woman's corpse being wheeled away. But he knew what had happened.

'Mrs Boswell died because she was old and it was, well, her time, I guess. But General Squeak...' She squatted to show Henry the tiny corpse. 'I think he climbed up on the sink. Dad must have left water in there after he shaved this morning. He drowned. I'm so sorry.' She couldn't bear to tell Henry the even more horrible truth.

The boy's mouth opened a little as he leaned towards the dead hamster, his eyes wide.

'Do you think they suffered?'

Reggie had not expected that question and she heard herself swallow, remembering the awful crackling of bone when she'd pulled General Squeak from the toilet, and the mask of horror that had frozen on Mrs Boswell's lifeless face.

'I don't think so,' Reggie lied.

Henry reached out a hand and stroked the hamster's head with an index finger. 'He looks so broken. All twisted up.'

Reggie bleated. She wasn't prepared for it and the sound came out like a gag. And then she started crying and she couldn't stop. She knelt there in the hallway, a dead rodent on a facecloth in her hands like some bizarre sacrifice.

'You're crying.'

Reggie looked up at her brother. He tilted his head slightly, and his blue eyes stared at her, cool and curious. He touched a tear on her cheek, dabbing it softly so that it pooled on his fingertip. He examined it like there was something alien about it, like it required study and dissection.

'Of course I'm crying. First Mrs Boswell, and now this? Aren't you sad, Henry? Don't you want to hold him?' She held the hamster out. 'Say goodbye?'

'I don't know what to say or what to do with it,' Henry said flatly. 'Now that it's dead.' His lip quivered, the first sign that he was feeling *something*. Reggie didn't press.

'Well, we need to find him a nice coffin.' She wiped away the streams of snot that had bubbled out of her nose. 'Something warm. Make him cozy inside. And then take him outside and bury him. Say a prayer and let his spirit go.'

Henry looked intrigued. He placed his hand on General Squeak's body. His finger squished into the corpse, and the furry skin gave like a sponge.

'Where does it go?' he asked matter-of-factly. 'The spirit?'

'To heaven, Henry.'

'Have you seen a spirit?'

'You can't see it. You feel it. Inside you.' She pointed to Henry's chest. 'In your heart. It's what makes you who you are.'

The boy stood still for a long moment and then turned away. 'I'm going to get a shoebox. You can bury it after I have waffles.'

'He didn't want to come out with you to bury it?' Aaron climbed off the rusty twelve-speed he'd owned since the seventh grade and joined Reggie, who was tromping through the unbroken snow of the side yard, carrying the shoebox coffin and a spade. 'That's harsh. Is he messed up bad, Reg?'

'Well, I broke some ribs pulling him out of the toilet, but he was dead by then.'

'No, not the hamster, dork. Henry. How's his head?'

Reggie's boots cracked the thin crust of ice and sank deep into the powder beneath. Aaron clomped awkwardly beside her.

'Bad,' said Reggie. 'He's so mixed up, Aaron. Like he needs to act all tough and hard now. He didn't even cry when he saw Squeak was dead.'

'I didn't cry when my cat got hit by a car.' It was true, but he'd wanted to. 'I was about Henry's age, but then again –'

'You're a natural tough guy.'

Aaron smirked. 'Yeah, well, you know me. Maybe I could talk to Henry. Guy to guy. Sounds lame, I know –'

'Would you do that?'

'Sure.' Aaron took the spade from Reggie as they trekked through the backyard. 'Here, let me do the honours.'

He cleared some snow away and then stabbed the spade into the icy ground. It was like digging into clay bricks. He didn't know if they could even get deep enough to cover the shoebox, but he didn't want to tell Reggie that. She seemed pretty set on the hamster's funeral plans.

'Is it totally frozen?' she asked.

'Well, let's just say this is going to take a while.'

From the corner of his eye, he noticed a shape in one of her house's windows. Henry stood in his second-floor bedroom, still as an ice sculpture, staring at them through a pane of cracked glass.

'Hey, Reggie? That creep you out a little?'

Reggie followed Aaron's gaze.

'I told you.' She sighed. 'He's acting weird. Like some gears aren't matching up right in there.'

'Let me see the hamster.'

'What for?'

Aaron grabbed the box from Reggie's hands and opened it. He lifted the hamster out of its cardboard coffin and turned it over, hoping his suspicions were wrong.

'And you found it in the toilet?' he asked.

'Yeah. Clogged it. Really jammed in.'

'Its neck's broken.' Aaron lifted the creature's head, examining how ruined the pathetic thing really was.

'Yeah. I told you, I broke a couple bones when I pulled him out, because –'

'I don't think that's how it happened. Look.' He pointed to the thin layer of skin that seemed to be the only thing keeping the head attached. 'Somebody, well –'

Aaron glanced back up at the window. Henry was no longer there.

'What are you doing here, Aaron?'

Henry had appeared on the back deck. Bound up in several layers of sweatshirts and then wrapped in Dad's green down parka, he looked like a lumpy zucchini. Aaron would have laughed if it weren't for the venom in the boy's voice.

'I came to pay my respects to General Squeak, Henry.' Aaron took the box from Reggie's hands and laid the hamster back inside. He closed the lid and gave it back to her, not taking his eyes off Henry. 'I'm really sorry about what happened, man. You okay?'

69

'Reggie's grounded. You better go home before my dad calls.' Henry pulled the parka collar tight round his neck as he turned to go indoors. 'He doesn't like you much.'

'Henry,' Reggie snapped. 'Back off! He's burying *your* pet.'

Aaron held a finger up to silence Reggie. He walked after Henry.

'Hey.'

Henry didn't stop.

'Hey, Henry, wait. Come on, bud, wait up a minute.'

The boy faced him with flaring eyes. 'I'm going inside. It's cold out here.'

Aaron squinted up at the bright sun. 'Not so bad. A little above freezing today, eh? And you like winter, big snowboarder that you are.'

'Yeah.' Henry just stood on the porch.

'Can you come down here a minute? I want to talk.'

The boy baulked but said nothing.

'Just for a minute. Please?'

Henry teetered down the deck steps. He stared at Aaron expectantly.

'Reggie's worried about you, Henry. Are you doing all right?'

'I'm fine.' Henry shook his head. 'Can I go now?' He started back up the steps, but Aaron reached out and grabbed his wrist.

'Come on. Just talk a sec. Did you have an *accident* with General Squeak?'

'Let go of me.' The command was calm and threatening. Henry's eyes locked with Aaron's, and the older boy felt a cold force closing in on him. Something inhuman lurked behind Henry's stare, and it held Aaron firmly in its grip.

70

Aaron struggled to look away, but he couldn't. Drowning in the child's blue gaze, his body wouldn't answer his mind. He was underwater, paralysed and suffocating. Sunlight faded; a tunnel closed in until there was blackness on all sides. His lungs burned. Henry's image rippled before him. Aaron couldn't breathe. The water rushed into his chest . . .

He coughed and gagged. There was no water, only the cold blue depths of Henry's eyes. Henry cracked a smile as Aaron fell to his knees in the snow, gasping for breath.

'Go home, Aaron. You're not welcome here.'

Henry laughed bitterly and walked away.

Aaron caught his breath. His pulse pounded with rage and fear. He snatched up a hunk of hard, icy snow and hurled it at Henry. It slammed into the back of his target's head.

'Aaron!' Reggie yelled. 'Chill out!'

Henry yelped and twisted. He growled and leaped at Aaron, knocking him on his back. His hands curled round Aaron's throat, and then the drowning sensation struck again, full force.

'Henry – *stop*!' Reggie screamed.

Aaron kicked and writhed, his lungs afire. Reggie grabbed Henry's shoulders, trying to prise him off.

'Henry! Leave him alone! STOP IT!'

Henry flailed, smacking the point of his elbow into Reggie's face, hitting just under her left eye. She gasped and staggered back.

Aaron clenched a fistful of snow and mashed it into Henry's face, making him shriek and jump away. Reggie dived to grab her brother round the waist, but he snapped forward and head-butted her in the nose. She fell to the ground like a sack of stones.

Aaron, his vision clouded with yellow dots, tried to focus. Henry's cheek and nose looked *seared* where the snow had hit him, like raw meat dropped in a hot skillet. Grey threads branched out from the blackened patches.

'*Jesus . . .*' Aaron gasped.

Henry covered his face with both hands and raced up the deck into the house.

Reggie lay perfectly still on the snow, warm blood gushing from her nose and staining the whiteness around her.

8

Reggie vaguely recalled clinging to Aaron as he furiously ped-alled his bike. 'Reggie, can you hear me? Don't let go!' Fogged with pain, she stayed upright and focused as best she could on her friend's voice.

She awoke with Eben's frowning face above her, his gentle hand holding the ice pack to her nose. Reggie grimaced, the skin beneath her eye puffy and tender. Aaron stood behind Eben, biting his lip in worry.

She reclined on a small Victorian fainting couch. Behind it stood a tall glass-fronted cabinet, filled with ancient-looking books. An orange cat with one pronounced fang stalked in the hall beyond. This was Eben's apartment above the bookstore.

'No broken bones, but you'll have some bruises,' Eben said.

Aaron leaned in.

'Merry Christmas, huh?' He smiled and stroked her hair. 'I didn't think you'd want to deal with my mother asking why your nose looks like a plum, so I came here.'

Reggie nodded. She tried to sit up, but dizziness forced her back down on the couch. Eben put a hand on her shoulder.

'Easy does it. We don't want the bleeding to start up again.'

'Where's Henry?' Reggie ran her tongue along her teeth and tasted the rusty, dried blood. Blurred images floated around in her brain. She turned to Aaron and saw the faint blue marks Henry's little hands had left on his neck. 'Oh, God. Are you okay?'

'I'm fine.' Aaron's hand reflexively went to his throat. He nodded. 'I guess Henry's still at home,' he said.

'Alone?'

'For now.'

'I have to go. My dad –' Reggie staggered to her feet. 'He'll kill me if he finds out I left Henry home alone, especially on Christmas Eve.'

'Sit down, Regina,' said Eben.

Reggie sank back down on the couch.

'Henry killed General Squeak,' said Aaron.

'I know.' Reggie swallowed hard. Her throat burned. 'I think I knew it before you did.'

'He needs to see someone, Reggie,' Eben said. 'I'm not trying to butt into your family's life, but if he's hurting people now . . .' He took off his glasses and wiped them with a cloth. 'You don't want this to escalate.'

'I know. He needs to see a shrink,' Reggie said.

'Henry needs more than a shrink.' Aaron picked up a glass of water from the coffee table, and the ice cubes clinked from the shaking of his hand. 'I think something happened to Henry after we read from that book the other night.'

'*The Devouring*? I read him a story from it. I've been thinking maybe that triggered bad memories.'

'No, Reg. Not memories.'

'Then what?'

74

'He's different now.' Aaron looked her straight in the eyes. 'I don't think he's your brother any more. I don't think he's Henry.'

Reggie choked out a laugh.

'Oh, yeah? Then who is he? Elvis?'

Aaron didn't smile.

'Wait. You're seriously thinking –? That's freaking great, Aaron. Thanks for that terrific rational approach. Now we're really getting somewhere.'

'I did the rational, and none of the answers make sense.'

'Slow down,' said Eben. 'Aaron, what are you saying?'

Reggie jabbed a finger at Aaron's chest.

'*The Devouring* is just a stupid book! A fairy tale, Aaron. Words, nothing more.'

'Words are written down for a reason. Was there a real Cyclops? No – but could there have been some big, ugly mother of a mutation with one eye? Yes.' He looked to Eben. 'You've read every book ever written. Do you understand what I mean?'

Eben considered Aaron's words.

'Are there nuggets of truth to incredible tales? Sure. But it's quite a leap to say that just because this book exists there are creatures from another dimension who steal children's souls. I don't think an inquisition is the next logical step here.'

'Just hear me out,' said Aaron. 'Henry's a kid who freaks out easy. If Vours *do* exist, if they attack those most afraid on Sorry Night, *Henry* would be the perfect victim, right?'

'I hate to say it, Aaron, but *you* weren't exactly a portrait of courage the other night. Why didn't they get you, then?'

'Because I wasn't all alone – and I didn't really believe in the Vours. Think about how they came for Jeremiah in the book. He was in the dark, by himself, and he knew about the things that come out on Sorry Night.'

'It wasn't total darkness. Jeremiah had a lantern below him,' Reggie corrected. As soon as she said it, she remembered the little night light at the end of Henry's bed, but decided not to mention it.

'The point is this was just a game to us,' Aaron said. 'But, to Henry, it was real.'

'So if I go home and chant "Bloody Mary" into my bedroom mirror three times, I'll have a gory corpse standing behind me, if I believe in her?' said Reggie. 'Great. Maybe she and Henry can go slaughter stray cats together.'

'Reggie, I saw things.'

'What things?'

'Henry's skin. Something happened when the snow touched it. It got . . . darker.'

'Like a rash?'

'No. Like a burn.'

'People have reactions to extreme cold, Aaron,' said Eben. He leaned forward to scratch his cat between the ears. 'It's not uncommon.'

'Henry's a snow rat! Have you ever seen him have an allergic reaction to snow, or ice, or the cold? Even once?' Reggie shook her head. 'Well, neither have I.'

'You said "things", ' said Reggie. 'What else did you see?'

'You're going to think I'm insane.'

'I'm already there.'

'When I fell on my knees? I fell because I couldn't breathe. I was drowning.'

'What?'

'Henry looked in my eyes and he knew what I was afraid of. I can't explain it, but he knew, and he made it real in my mind.'

Eben stood up.

'That's enough. You're both upset –'

Aaron slammed his palms against the table; the sudden noise sent the cat scampering under the couch.

'There's something *in* him, damn it! I saw it!'

'What did you see, Aaron?' asked Eben. 'Describe it.'

'We were face-to-face, and I saw *something* behind his eyes.'

Reggie scowled.

'Here's what I think. You think you saw something, and I don't blame you. He was choking you and you freaked. But fear does strange things, and the truth is you're scared of your own shadow.'

Seeing the look on Aaron's face, Reggie instantly regretted what she'd said.

'I didn't mean that.'

'Yes, you did, and I don't care. I'm a coward, fine. But I'm not a fool, Reg. I know what I saw. And I'm willing to bet Mrs Boswell saw something too. Henry showed her something that literally scared her to death.'

'First my brother's a demon, and now he murders little old ladies?' Reggie stood and strode towards the doorway. 'I'm leaving.'

Aaron grabbed her arm as she passed him. 'Don't trust anything he says. Stay away from him tonight. Even if you just get spooked, call me and I'll come over.'

Reggie wrenched her arm free and headed down the stairs.

She stepped out onto the sidewalk and focused on putting one foot in front of the other. She didn't want to *think*. Her mind was like some medieval castle, with her hope locked up inside and Aaron's words laying siege to it. *I don't think he's your brother any more . . . I don't think he's Henry . . .*

A red Mustang slowed to a growling crawl beside her. The window rolled down, and Quinn called to her from behind the wheel.

'Hey, Halloway!' His smile quickly fell. 'Whoa, what happened to your nose?'

Reggie's hand flew to her face. She'd forgotten she looked like a punching bag. 'Sledding accident,' she said.

Oh, fantastic. What fifteen-year-old still went sledding?

'Was it contact sledding? Let me give you a ride home.'

Reggie smiled gratefully and reached for the passenger side door just as her father's pickup pulled up behind Quinn's car. He rolled his window down, and Reggie could smell his anger.

'Get in.'

9

Dad barely talked on the ride home, except to ask what on earth Reggie had done to her face. She said she had slipped on some ice.

As they drove, Reggie realized she had no love for the season any more. Her mom was gone, her dad no longer trusted her, and her brother . . . well, Aaron thought her brother was a Vour. All the cheesy lights, recycled carols and plastic reindeer around Cutter's Wedge just reinforced her faithlessness in anything redemptive about the holidays.

'If I didn't think it would ruin Christmas for the family, I'd ground you through New Year's,' Dad finally said.

'The family. Right.'

'Don't push it, Regina.'

'Ground me. What've I got to celebrate? More laundry?'

They pulled into the driveway and Dad cut the engine. Reggie opened the door and stepped out.

'Drop the attitude, Reggie. This is tough for all of us. Doesn't help the situation if you —'

'Sorry, Dad. I've got trousers to iron.' She slammed the car door and marched into the house.

79

Upstairs, Reggie noticed hot steam escaping beneath the bathroom door. Henry was in the bathtub singing 'Deck the Halls'. For a moment she thought about confronting him, but then remembered what Aaron had told her.

Stay away from him tonight.

So she went straight to her room and closed the door. Lying in bed, she felt the blood thumping in her bruised face. She heard Henry's bare feet running down the hallway, followed by Dad's heavy footsteps. Through the heating vent in the wall, Reggie heard their bedtime chat.

'You get some sleep now, little man,' Dad said.

'I know.' Henry sighed. 'Santa won't come until I'm asleep.'

'Funny to hear you say that. Last year you told me you didn't believe in Santa Claus.'

'I changed my mind.'

'Oh, yeah?'

'Well, just because you can't see something doesn't mean it isn't real.'

'That's exactly right. Goodnight, Henry.'

Reggie heard Dad leave the room. She lay with her eyes closed, the wind tapping against her window. An image of the mangled hamster lying in the shoebox came to her.

'Reggie . . .' Her brother's voice was a whisper. 'Reggie, I'm sorry about today.'

She opened her eyes and turned her head. A short silhouette stood in her doorway. The pitiful Kappy dangled from his hand.

'How could you do that to Aaron?'

'I said I was sorry, didn't I?'

'How could you *do* that?'

She could hear him breathing. She thought she saw him smile.

'He started it.'

'Henry, what's happened to you? Is something going on at school? Are you getting picked on?'

'I do the picking now.' His voice was gravelly, and cold surged through Reggie at his words.

'What do you mean?' she asked slowly. Henry just swung Kappy back and forth. A piece of stuffing fluttered to the floor.

'I got some presents for you, Reggie. I think you'll like them.'

The silhouette disappeared back down the dark hall, and Reggie heard Henry's door close. She rose and shut her own door.

Ever since Sorry Night, life had gone from difficult to dismal. When she had first borrowed *The Devouring*, it seemed twisted and fun. Now, she recalled its pages as emanations of darkness and madness. She regretted ever picking it up.

It's not possible . . .

Something moved to her left. A spider was crawling down the wall. It might have been the one Aaron had released from the jar on Sorry Night, mottled brown and fat, but it seemed larger. Bumpy skin stretched tight over the meaty bulk of its abdomen. Thick fang-tipped appendages, moist with venom, twitched in the centre of its face. Its segmented legs, bristling with hair, rose and fell with sickening undulation as it crept closer. Eight tiny black eyes gleamed at her through the darkness. Reggie knew it couldn't be possible, but she thought she heard it breathing. Terror bloomed inside her, freezing her, clogging her throat.

Something scratched and rattled behind the vent near the ceiling. Her gaze snapped up to the sound, and she saw the tips of innumerable spider legs poking through the grate. The vent creaked and shifted in its moorings. The spider on the wall hissed, and a creature beyond the vent replied, and then another, and another, multiplying the sound until a horrid rasping chorus filled the room. The vent's cover burst open and clattered to the floor.

A mass of scrambling legs and dripping fangs poured down the wall and flooded onto the floor like a dark boiling slime.

Reggie scrambled to the door, only to find that the knob would not turn. She yanked it desperately until a hairy brown spider crawled through the keyhole and made for her fingers. Flailing and stumbling, she headed for the window, but dozens of spiders dropped from the sill and crept around the curtains.

Helpless, Reggie tried to dive under her covers, but spiders flooded into her bed from all sides, spinning down from the ceiling on sticky white threads or crawling out of the pillowcases. She realized she was screaming, but the shrieks were so piercing and uncontrollable that they seemed to be coming from somewhere else, somewhere that had been hidden deep inside of her . . . until now. She yanked the blanket from her bed, sending spiders scattering in all directions, then pulled it over her head. The world darkened around her. Amid the crawling chaos, she heard someone calling for her.

'Reggie!'

A firm grip snatched the blanket and pulled it from her head and shoulders. She looked up to see a man-sized spider rearing up before her; it stood on four of its thick arachnid legs. The other four wrapped around her arms, grasping her at the wrists and elbows. Cold spiny hair bristled against her skin. The spider's fangs clacked and oozed. Deafened by shock, she saw her silently screaming face reflected in each of the spider's glinting black eyes. It raised its head to strike . . .

'REGINA!'

Reggie blinked and saw her father's reddened face as she struggled in his grasp. She leaped away from him and ripped the sheets off her bed. She gibbered incoherently as she shook her pillows and checked under the mattress, but there was nothing there. Sweat-soaked and trembling, she turned to face her father.

'There were spiders everywhere.' Her whisper was dry and brittle. 'Dad, you have to believe me! The vent cover popped off, and, Dad, I swear, so many of them just swarmed in. I *felt* them on me!'

He looked up to the vent. It was intact.

'I don't see anything, Reggie. You were just dreaming. But it's all right – you're awake now.'

Reggie clutched her head. Henry walked into the room, rubbing his eyes and yawning.

'What's going on?' he asked.

'Keep away from me!' Reggie shouted.

Dad put a hand on her shoulder.

'Reggie, it's just Henry.'

'He made the spiders! He made the spiders come after me!' Even in her terror, she knew it sounded childish – or totally insane.

'Is she okay, Dad?'

'GET OUT!' she shrieked.

'Henry,' Dad said softly. 'Go back to bed, okay?'

The boy shrugged and walked out. Reggie felt hot stinging tears begin to flow, and soft sobs trembled out of her lips.

Her father patted her awkwardly on the back.

'It will be okay, Reggie. We're going to be okay.'

She stared at the empty doorway. Aaron's words seeped into her mind: *Henry looked in my eyes and he knew what I was afraid of. I can't explain it, but he knew – and he made it real in my mind.*

'You're right,' she said, wiping away her tears. 'I'm fine. It was a dream.'

Reggie climbed back into bed, and her father kissed her forehead. But, hours after he'd gone, Reggie still lay awake, her rational mind battling the terrible seeds of a growing obsession.

10

Christmas morning arrived and Reggie tried to be gracious about the clothes and gift certificates she received, but her eyes kept returning to Henry. He gleefully ripped the wrapping paper from his presents, shouting about how much he loved everything. Dad smiled at his exuberance; Reggie hadn't seen her father that pleased in a long while.

She was dreading the annual Halloway trip into Boston for a lobster lunch at Faneuil Hall. Minus one mother this year. Reggie would've rather had her fingernails pulled out with pliers. Especially when she saw that Dad had put on the ugly Christmas sweater with the velvet reindeer on it.

'I'm not going,' she told her father.

'It's *Christmas*, Regina. You're going.'

Reggie walked defiantly to the stairs. 'Bye,' she said, not looking back at him. The yelling she expected to follow her upstairs never came. Dad didn't say a thing. He just slammed the door behind him.

'Merry Christmas, Reggie!' called Henry.

Reggie went to the window. She watched them get in the car and back out of the driveway. Henry gazed up at her and waved.

Back in the hallway she found shreds of paper on the carpet. She picked up a few scraps of a torn photograph, the picture of their family at the Bottle Hill carnival.

Henry had ripped it up and left the pieces for her.

Her eyes filled with tears. She was losing him. She felt him slipping from her, and the loss was worse than the abandonment by their mother. Mom had packed a bag and left, gone of her own free will. But Henry . . . Henry was being *taken* from her, a little more day by day, like someone with a terminal disease.

She got dressed and was out of the house three minutes later.

Soon after, Reggie and Aaron were knocking on Eben's door. He answered it a few moments later, his eyes squinting at them through the morning sun.

'Sorry,' Reggie said. 'I know it's Christmas, but we –'

'Come on in. Coffee's almost ready.'

Aaron's 1940s leather aviator hat with long earflaps made him look like a bloodhound. He eyed Eben's ancient bathrobe. 'Nice duds.'

'Thank you. Nice hat.'

'Hanukkah present. Told the folks I was wearing it to Reggie's annual Christmas morning breakfast. I sort of lied, but I figured we'd be getting breakfast here, right?'

'You're lucky to get a bad cup of coffee.'

They all sat at the kitchen table and Aaron poured himself a huge mug of coffee. He drank more caffeine than anyone Reggie had ever met. It explained why he was rail thin, jumpy and usually pretty sweaty. Even in winter. But she figured with a brain that ran as hot as his did, constant fuel was a necessity more than a habit.

'All right. You all can start talking any time you like.'

'Spiders,' said Reggie. 'I was ambushed.'

'Spiders?' asked Eben.

'Not real ones,' said Aaron. 'The *psychic* kind, courtesy of Henry. Like when he made me think I was drowning.'

'My room was dripping with them. Thousands of them.'

Eben listened without expression.

'So now you believe your brother is a Vour?'

Reggie shook her head.

'I don't know what to believe, Eben. It's preposterous, but – I *don't* know the kid sleeping in the room next to mine any more.'

Eben frowned and rubbed his unshaven chin. A coughing fit seized him, and he put a hand on the table to steady himself.

'Jeez, Eben.'

'It sounds worse than it is,' Eben assured her. 'Now, let's take a look at the facts of this situation for a moment –'

Aaron pulled a thick three-ring binder from his backpack and thumped it onto the end table.

'What do you have there?' Eben asked.

With a flourish, Aaron flipped the binder open to reveal a computer-printed copy of the handwritten title page: *The Devouring*.

'You made a copy of it?' Reggie whispered. 'When?'

'I scanned it into my laptop the night I borrowed it. Thought maybe I could research the symbols and stuff –'

'You two just couldn't leave well enough alone, could you?' Eben said in a sharp voice.

'Don't blame Reggie. She didn't know. Be angry with me if

87

you want, but we've got to find out where this came from,' Aaron said.

'And how do you plan to do that?' asked Eben. 'It's only a journal. No publishing data, no Library of Congress number, no copyright . . .'

Aaron paged through the binder.

'We read the whole thing, word by word. There's got to be *something* in here that gets us *somewhere*.' Aaron turned to the first page and shook his empty coffee mug. 'I'll need more joe.'

Aaron was over halfway through the journal and had lost track of how many cups of coffee he'd drunk. Eben was reading one of his psychology textbooks on delusional dementia while Reggie slept in a tall wingback chair, a thin strand of spittle hanging from the corner of her mouth.

Aaron's eyes slid back and forth over the handwritten text.

'Listen to this,' he said. '*They know I know, and they torment me. They force in the nightmares. One moment I'm at the market, the next I'm sinking in quicksand, screaming, struggling. And the humans – all they do is stare. Stare and whisper at crazy Macie.* Macie. That's the author. And what happened to her is just like what happened to us. Vours sense your fears, then they play them out for you in your head, like waking nightmares.'

'Or you subconsciously remember reading this passage, and it's affecting your ability to judge reality from fantasy,' said Eben.

'I don't know, Eben, it felt pretty real,' said Reggie, rubbing her eyes and wiping her lips. Aaron continued flipping through the book.

'Here's something . . . maybe.' He jabbed a finger at the page.

'*Twelfth of May 1972. Went to see Ma and Pa. Brought Ma a bunch of daisies and told them Jeremiah was getting real sick.*'

'Okay. She visits her folks . . . and Vour-possessed people can get sick. So?'

'There's more.' Aaron read on. '*They got a new neighbour. I knew the boy from school years ago. A bad seed. He went to prison for burning down St Luke's with Father Moore and those kids inside back in '54. I always thought he was a Vour.*'

Aaron flipped back to the account of Jeremiah in the cornfield.

'Right here on page one, the night the Vours got Jeremiah,' he said, and read aloud again. '*He never used to have a mean bone in his body. I think that after Ma died, some part of him did too.*' Aaron stood up. 'Their mother was *dead* before the journal even existed! You get it now?'

'Get to the point,' said Reggie. She shot a look at Eben, who seemed deep in thought.

Aaron paced. 'She brought Ma a bunch of daisies. She's talking about a cemetery. She went to visit their *graves*!'

'So?' asked Reggie, but Eben nodded to himself.

'We have a *date*,' he said. 'Twelfth of May 1972. We have a singular *event* – the church burning – that happened about twenty years before. And we can almost certainly find the story, the killer's name and his hometown, at the library or on the web.'

'And he's buried next to Jeremiah's parents,' said Reggie.

Aaron sat before Eben's computer.

'Their tombstones will give us the author's last name. That might get us an address!'

'Probably true,' Eben replied. 'But I don't know what you hope to find. You don't even know if she's still alive, or if the passing years have only added to her insanity.'

'"Madness in great ones must not unwatched go",' said Aaron, typing like a demon.

'Don't quote Shakespeare at me, young man,' Eben said. 'You're talking about hunting monsters.'

Reggie had remained silent for a long while. Now she spoke.

'I don't know if I believe in monsters, Eben. But I know something is very wrong with Henry. And I'm scared for him. I'll be glad to prove that Vours don't exist, and this is some crazy stage my brother is going through. But if it's not a stage –'

'You want to visit a murderer's grave on Christmas?'

Both Reggie and Aaron looked expectantly at Eben.

'No. I know what you're thinking.' Eben shook his head and coughed. 'Absolutely not.'

'I could ask Quinn,' Reggie said. 'Kind of a weird first date, but he said he wants to spend some more time with me. Or I could just hitchhike . . .'

Reggie glared at Eben, and he sighed.

'Fine, Regina.' He grabbed his coat. 'But I've got a game hen to roast this evening, so let's make this foolish quest a quick one.'

11

The drive in Eben's old Cadillac took just under an hour. Aaron had found a treasure trove of information about the Garney incident online, and Reggie studied the printouts as they travelled.

On 2 February 1954, one Joseph Garney had set fire to a country church with the priest and a Sunday school class of five trapped inside. Eighteen years later, he died in prison. His body was shipped back to his hometown of Fredericks, a farm town at the foot of the Berkshire Mountains, in a plain pine box.

During the ride, Reggie felt an ember of hope flicker to life inside her. After they pulled into the local petrol station and learned there was only one cemetery in Fredericks, it flared even brighter.

When they found the place and drove through the open gates of the cemetery, Eben started coughing, a painful, sticky hack that forced him to pull to the side of the poorly ploughed road. Tombstones dotted the slopes, and a few bleak mausoleums stood on the crests.

'You okay?' Reggie patted Eben gently on the back.

'Fine, fine.'

'Stay here where it's warm. We'll be back in a few.'

Eben just held his white handkerchief to his mouth and nodded.

Reggie and Aaron got out of the car and surveyed the grounds.

'You start at the top row and work your way down,' Reggie said. 'I'll take the bottom one and work up.'

Aaron nodded.

'*Joseph Garney*,' he whispered. 'We'll find him.'

The muddy snow beneath Reggie's feet pulled at her boots, making a crunch-sucking sound with every step.

Louise Wilkes. Hollis Johnson. Charlotte Mundt . . .

She trudged onwards, trespassing in the land of the dead, imagining creatures of desiccated skin and mouldering bone seething beneath her feet.

. . . Hugo Branz. Katherine Stahl. Miriam Lukowski . . .

So many graves. So many stones.

. . . Simon Hastings. Bette Youmans. Fiona O'Connell . . .

This is what awaited everyone.

. . . Beloved Father, Cherished Wife, Dear Son . . .

Could Henry already be dead? If he wasn't in his body, then where was he? Where had the Vours taken him?

Shivering, Reggie knelt in front of a small, nondescript stone caked in grime and frost. She cleared the stone and saw the epitaph:

Pray God Forgive Him
Joseph Garney, 1935 – 1972

'Aaron! Down here!'

Aaron scrambled down the slope as Reggie started clearing away snow from an adjacent headstone.

By the time Aaron reached her, Reggie had uncovered the name:

Joanna Canfield
1901 – 1929
Beloved Mother

Aaron scraped the ice from the stone right beside it, revealing the name of Joshua Canfield, who died and was buried beside his wife a decade later.

'Canfield,' said Aaron. 'These have to be Macie's parents, right?'

Reggie nodded. 'Macie Canfield. She's our girl.'

Aaron placed his hand on her shoulder. 'Now let's go find her.'

Eben looked tired when they returned to the car, but his coughing had calmed. He smiled when they told him Macie's full name.

'Now we can find her, Eben!' Aaron shouted. 'All we need –'

'Tomorrow.'

'But we're so close. All we need is –'

'Aaron,' Eben said, 'it's *Christmas*. Everything is closed. Libraries, post offices, courthouses . . .'

'So tomorrow.'

12

Early the next morning, Reggie's dad didn't yell at her. He didn't speak a word to her. He wouldn't even look at her when she passed him in the kitchen. The sad silence made it unbearable, and she wanted to take his hands in hers, to talk to him, to make him hear the truth. But it wouldn't do any good. Reggie was like a phantom to him.

But right now she had Henry to worry about.

She grabbed a bagel and some orange juice, and then walked to Aaron's house. They scoured the web all morning together, but it offered few clues. Eben drove them back to Fredericks at noon, to the courthouse there, but records of land deeds were still kept in paper files (and in complete disarray).

Finally, a visit to the local postmaster provided the address, though he gave Eben a strange look when he asked about the Canfield place. Mail had stopped going there years ago. Aaron bounced in the back seat of the Cadillac like a child going to the beach, but Reggie and Eben were solemn.

Few street signs existed in Fredericks, so they spent the better part of an hour doubling back in search of the mailboxes or forked oak trees to which the postmaster had directed them.

When they at last arrived on the lonely road at the edge of town, a coldness gripped the place, even though they were snug inside Eben's heated car. The wintertime forest looked monochromatic, black on white, as if something had sucked the warmth and colour from the world. Eben coughed and hacked up some phlegm.

'You sound terrible,' said Reggie.

'I get this thing every winter. It lasts a week and then goes away.' Eben took out his handkerchief and dabbed his red nose. 'Don't worry about me.'

As they rolled down the forest road, the tarmac beneath broke up and turned to icy dirt. Snow had drifted over the lane in parts, but Eben expertly navigated the treacherous roads, driving his Caddie like a professional wheelman. The forest grew denser as they progressed, the undergrowth more twisted and thorny. Beyond the trees hung the white and empty sky. They were on their way to the *end* of somewhere.

They came to a clearing. The hole in the woods around them seemed sudden and strange, as if it had been the site of a meteor impact or a toxic spill. An old, decrepit house sat below the road, halfway down a slope leading to acres of flat, snow-shrouded land. Its cracked cedar shingles looked like skin mottled with lesion-like clumps of rot. Half of the chimney had crumbled away. The hill was littered with its stones.

Eben stopped the car. 'Remember. If there's anybody here, *I* start things off. Right?'

Reggie nodded, and they all got out. No birds chirped, no dogs barked, no animals chattered. A metal mailbox, shaped like a barn, lay on the roadside, half-covered with frost. All the

letters of the name had peeled off, but the outline remained:
M. CANFIELD.

'Guess we're at the right place,' said Reggie. She flipped the little door open. There was nothing inside.

They made their way down the slope and stepped onto the decaying porch. A rusty wind chime hung silent and lifeless in the still air. Four empty bird feeders were suspended from the eaves. Aaron nudged one with a finger, and it creaked on its wire.

'Somebody likes birds.'

Reggie peered inside through a window. The curtains were threadbare, but thick enough that she could only see outlines of the things on the other side.

Eben knocked on the front door. Nothing stirred inside. Reggie pounded on it and twisted the knob, but it was locked.

'*Ahem.*' Eben cleared his throat. 'What are you doing? Trespassing is one thing, but breaking and entering is quite another.'

Aaron pointed to the door's windowpane. It had a crack down its centre.

'Looks already broken to me.' Aaron took off his scarf and wrapped his fist with it.

'Aaron,' Eben said, 'don't –'

Aaron punched the glass. Reggie looked at Eben.

'I know you don't approve. But I have to know I've done everything I can to help Henry.'

'This isn't research, Regina,' he said, shaking his head. 'This is burglary.'

'He's my little brother, Eben. Even the slightest clue would be worth it.'

Aaron stuck his hand through the pane, clutched the inside knob and opened the door. The trio stepped inside and into a kingdom of cobwebs. A wave of foul, dead air greeted them.

'Jeez . . .'

'Hello?' Reggie hollered. 'Anyone here?'

Aaron flicked the light switch. Nothing happened.

Pale light streamed through the grimy windows. Rusty food cans littered a small kitchen to their right – on the table, the floor, piled in the sink. The refrigerator and stove were relics, the sort of old appliances that looked as though you'd need a crane to move them, or a wrecking ball to destroy them.

'Real neat freak,' said Aaron. He picked up a can and wiped the dust from the label. 'Canned peaches.'

Eben shone a flashlight around what looked to be a dining room. A few large sacks of something were piled on the table. He walked over to examine them.

'What's for dinner over there?' Reggie called.

'Cement mix,' he answered. 'It seems Miss Canfield never got around to fixing up that chimney.'

Reggie picked up a butterfly net from beside a rotting sofa. She plucked out a feather from the ragged netting.

Aaron came into the room holding a wooden baseball bat he'd found. He gave it a swing or two. 'Eben, shine the light over here.'

The bat was crusted with something dark and reddish brown.

'Now what does that look like to you?' asked Aaron.

Reggie took a step towards the opposite doorway and stopped. At her feet were the shrivelled remains of a bird. The feathers looked like they had once been blue.

'Gross.'

'Must have come down the chimney and couldn't get out,' Aaron said.

The light was much dimmer in the next room. Reggie felt blindly as she stepped through the doorway. Something dry and brittle crunched under her foot. She took another step, and the toe of her sneaker sent a mass of small things scattering across the floor.

'Eben, I'm stepping on something . . .'

He shone the flashlight into the room.

'Oh, God . . .' whispered Reggie.

Little bones blanketed the living room floor. Aaron bent down and picked up a tiny rib cage.

Eben panned the light around.

At the far end of the room was a mountain of feathers of every size and colour, enough to fill dozens of garbage bags.

'Birds,' Aaron said.

Aaron walked towards the feathers, the bones crunching beneath his boots. 'I don't think they all came down the chimney.'

'My guess is those bird feeders were the bait,' Eben said. 'Someone caught them with the net –'

'And killed them with the bat,' Aaron finished.

'But . . . why?' Reggie asked. 'Some kind of Vour defence ritual?'

'Maybe,' said Aaron. He picked up a feather and twirled it in his fingers. 'Or she could have eaten them.'

'Ew, that's just nasty,' said Reggie.

'Ran out of peaches.'

'But there are supermarkets fifteen minutes away.'

'Macie was too scared to leave her place, remember?'

They searched the house, moving quickly. They opened every drawer and cabinet. Dug under every cushion. The bedroom had a stained, prehistoric mattress that Eben lobbied against anyone touching, but Reggie lent Aaron one of her gloves and they dragged it off the frame. There was nothing underneath it.

Back in the living room, Eben pushed aside one of the mildewed curtains and looked at the dimming sky. 'It's going to get dark soon, and we've got a bit of driving ahead of us.'

'But there has to be something here besides bird bones!' Reggie kicked the pile of bones and scattered them everywhere.

Aaron pointed at her feet. 'Look at the floor!'

There was something embedded in the wood. It had a dull shine of very old metal. Eben leaned forward to get a better look.

'It's a hinge,' he said.

Reggie and Aaron kicked away the bones, hacking and coughing as dust filled their lungs. After clearing a space, they stared silently at a double-hinged door set in the floor with a recessed ring handle.

'A cellar,' Reggie said. She reached for the handle.

'Wait,' said Eben. He went back into the kitchen and returned with the bat. He handed it to Aaron, then grabbed the handle and yanked, showing a strength Reggie hadn't seen before. When the door opened, air moaned down the dark passage, as if the room below had been holding its breath for years. Wooden steps led into blackness.

'How did you do that?' asked Reggie.

'The cane fools most people,' Eben said. 'But only parts of me are frail.'

Reggie grabbed the flashlight and started down. Each step groaned under her weight, as if protesting her intrusion. The air was rank and tomblike, the darkness unnaturally thick. When she reached the bottom, the flashlight's beam seemed feeble and dying.

Aaron and Eben followed Reggie down the hole and joined her in the middle of a near-empty room. There were no boxes of keepsakes stacked on the dirt floor, no old trunks filled with letters and manuscripts. A wooden chair stood against the far wall, with a ratty coat hanging on its back. A metal washtub sat in the corner.

'Nothing. Absolutely nothing,' Reggie said.

'I'm sorry, Regina, but what did you expect to find?' Eben asked. 'Macie was a troubled woman. That's all. Will you now accept that Vours aren't real?'

Reggie didn't answer. Eben was right; she couldn't believe that for a moment she'd actually thought these storybook monsters existed. Maybe she was just going crazy.

'Give me the flashlight for a second,' Aaron said.

Reggie handed it to him. He crossed the room, leaned over the washtub and reached behind it. When he stood up, he held a trowel in his other hand.

'The tub's full of dry cement,' he said. 'What was she doing, you think?'

'You're talking about a woman who played home-run derby with birds, ate them and turned the bones into home decor,' said Reggie. 'It's not like she made logical choices exactly.'

'Sure,' said Aaron, 'but even wackjobs have their reasons.' He continued his exploration. Eben pulled his own coat tighter.

'It's getting colder down here.' He put his hands together and blew on them. 'Aaron, exactly what are you doing?'

Aaron straightened up, raising the beam of light. He touched the wall at eye level, moving his fingers across it in a straight line. He rapped his knuckles against it.

'Come here,' he said.

Reggie stepped closer. Aaron tapped the concrete again.

'It sounds hollow,' said Reggie.

'No more than a few inches thick. And this section here' – he traced a small square area with his finger – 'is patched, like someone covered up a hole. Here, hold this for me.'

He handed Reggie the flashlight. Then, without warning, he slammed the bat against the wall. A crack formed in the middle of the patch. Aaron smashed the wall again and again, each stroke harder and wilder. 'It'll give. I can feel it!'

The concrete crumbled and fell, leaving a sixty-centimetre hole in the wall. Reggie raised the light, and the three gathered close and peered inside.

Fifteen centimetres back was a second wall, coated with dust.

'Another wall. What is this place?' said Reggie. She flashed the light up and down. In some places where the dust wasn't as thick, it reflected back.

'It's glass,' said Aaron.

'Like a window?' asked Reggie.

She reached in and rubbed away the dust, revealing glass panes etched with an elaborate network of silvery lines and indecipherable lettering. She held the flashlight to the window.

Aaron yelped and jumped back. Eben caught his breath and coughed again.

Reggie didn't make a sound. Ice-cold fear flooded her body, but she didn't turn away. This was why she had come.

She was looking into another room, half the size of the room in which she stood. Reggie recognized giant versions of some of the symbols she'd seen in the journal, now scrawled in chalk all across the walls and floor. Two metres behind the window, a man sat in a rocking chair, dressed in the tattered remnants of a flannel suit and dress shoes. His wrists and ankles were lashed to the chair with heavy cord. A dusty Bible rested on his lap, and the little that was left of his decayed flesh clung to his bones in shreds. His jaw hung open in what was either a death's grin or his final scream.

Eben and Aaron peered over her shoulder.

'*In pace requiescat*,' Eben muttered.

'My God,' Reggie said. 'It's like Poe's "Cask of Amontillado", except for real.'

'Or that woman they found on a meat hook in your bookstore, Eben.'

'No. Someone put him in there *alive*,' Reggie whispered. 'And strapped him down. And sealed him in.'

'And made a window so they could sit and watch him die,' added Aaron.

'This has gone too far. Let's go,' said Eben. 'This isn't a game any more.'

Reggie shifted on her feet, and the changing angle of the flashlight made something gleam on the corpse. Reggie hadn't noticed it before.

'Aaron, come closer, look at this.'

'No way!'

'Aaron, for God's sake – he's dead! He's *more* than dead!'

Aaron grumbled and leaned towards the window.

'Look,' Reggie said.

'Reg, I already –'

'Look at his *chest*.'

Aaron squinted through the glass. Hanging on a chain round the corpse's neck, resting against his breastbone, was a round, silver medallion. It depicted a bearded man holding an arrow.

A St Giles medal.

Aaron's lips parted, but he said nothing.

'Now we know what happened to Jeremiah,' said Reggie.

'How do you know this is Jeremiah?' asked Eben.

'The medal. He always wore it.'

Eben frowned.

'Reggie, just because this poor soul wore a religious token –'

Aaron stabbed a finger at the window.

'Come on, Eben! When will you start believing? This house belonged to *Macie Canfield*! Jeremiah was her brother! The Vours got him – she saw the whole thing and wrote it down!'

'You shouldn't believe a stranger's story so easily,' Eben replied. 'Maybe this man died because of Macie's delusions, and maybe you're heading down the same road she did.'

'Reggie, tell him that – Reggie?'

Reggie stared into the chamber. Something hovered on the ceiling over the dead body, a moving shadow. But when she looked at it directly, it dissipated like steam in the wind.

Reggie whispered, 'Something else is in there.' She shone the light at the room's ceiling.

The shadow darkened.

'It looks like *smoke*,' said Aaron. 'No, wait. You don't think it's . . .'

Black vapour formed, rolling in on itself like burning paper. It was thicker and denser than smoke. Reggie, Aaron and Eben watched it meld into an oily cloud, roiling as it grew ever darker.

'Move away from the glass, Regina,' Eben whispered with urgency. 'Do it now.'

'Is it – I mean – could it be one of them? The thing from the cornfield?' Aaron asked. The bat trembled in his hand.

'It can't get out,' Reggie said. 'Macie imprisoned it. She did it. She caught the monster that took her brother.'

'You don't know what this thing can do,' Eben said. 'Please back away, now.'

Aaron's voice shook, and he stepped back. 'Reggie, come on.'

He pulled on her sleeve, but she shook him off. She couldn't take her eyes from the swirling smoke; it undulated with some sort of sickening purpose, something too dark and cold to call 'life'.

The baseball bat dropped from Aaron's hand and clattered to the floor. 'I can't . . . I can't . . .' he mumbled as he backed away. He tripped at the base of the stairs and then dashed up them like a fleeing animal.

Reggie's body felt leaden. Eben touched her hand.

'Regina, step away from the glass.'

'No.'

Her gaze locked on the window. Above them, Aaron's footsteps crushed bones as he raced through the living room.

'Regina . . .' Eben pleaded.

'Something's going to happen.'

The cloud fumed and churned over the corpse, seeming to pull the flashlight's beam into itself and devour it.

'Regina, I –'

'Go with Aaron! I'm staying!'

The chair inside the glass rocked, and Jeremiah's skull moved back and forth on its skeletal neck, as if it were nodding at her, saying *Yes, it's all true.*

The skull snapped off, rolled down the chest, bounced off a knee, and shattered into pieces on the floor.

A face emerged from the smoke, a relief in the vapour. The features melted and reformed. It settled into the countenance of a sad, young boy, and spoke with a voice of rustling leaves.

'*Let me devour your fear.*'

A piercing chill swept across Reggie's body. Nausea seized her.

The boy's face twisted into something inhuman – vicious, pitiless. Its sooty maw opened, tendrils of smoke wafted out like vipers, and a deep inhuman voice called to them.

'*Let . . . me . . . out.*'

Pulsing vibrations coursed through the room, thick with madness and hate, making Reggie clench her jaw and wobble on her feet.

'Can you feel it, Eben?' she asked.

'Yes. I –' He coughed and cleared his throat. He tried to take a breath, but doubled over, gasping.

'Eben!'

Another violent spasm sent him to his knees. Reggie dropped the flashlight as she knelt in front of him. She grabbed his shoulders.

'Breathe!'

The coughing stopped, and he gulped in some air.

'I'm okay.' He raised his head. Blood trickled out of the corner of his mouth.

'Eben . . .'

Eben raised a hand to his lips and blanched at his crimson fingertips. He took another breath, but it caught in his chest.

'Oh, no . . . Eben . . .'

He erupted in a wrenching, jagged cough, and a torrent of blood spewed from his mouth, splashing his shirt and the floor. Reggie screamed. Eben gasped and gagged, reeling back before his body stiffened and jackknifed over again. His jaws opened wide, and a thick red gush splattered at Reggie's feet; it gathered in an expanding wet heap of ropy organs and gore. She stood frozen in shock as Eben convulsed. Damp pink lungs slithered from his mouth and hung like fleshy pendulums from his chin.

Something grabbed her by the shoulders and spun her around.

'Regina!' Eben shouted. 'Can you hear me?'

She blinked rapidly and saw her old friend standing before her. The blood was gone.

It had been a nightmare, a waking nightmare.

It was the Vour.

'We're getting out of here – *now*,' said Eben.

She felt defiled . . . *violated*.

Through the window, the smoky face stared at her. There was

an intelligence at work behind the glass. Venomous and clever. Cruel. She saw the faint curl of a smile on the thing's lips. It had sensed her fears, rummaged through them, and played one out for her in her head. The eyes gleamed hatefully.

The face caved in on itself, like bones giving way. The whole of it whirled into a vortex, fuelled by a growing fury. The chair rocked faster and faster until the corpse collapsed: neck, clavicle, scapulae, ribs, sternum – one after another the bones tumbled to the floor in a heap. The skeleton's forearms, hands and shins remained tied to the chair.

The frenzied, smoky Vour whipped around its prison until it suddenly rushed at the window.

'LET – ME – OUT!'

It smashed into the glass and burst into bits of smoke. And then it was gone.

Reggie's entire body quaked. Eben put his arm round her and helped her up the stairs.

Aaron huddled by the front tyre of the Cadillac with his head in his hands. When he saw Eben and Reggie coming towards him, he jumped to his feet.

'Reggie, I'm sorry, I –'

'Get in the car,' said Eben.

Reggie lay down in the back seat and Eben drove away from the house. Aaron reached back from the front seat and took Reggie's hand, but he couldn't say anything. Reggie's tears had left thin, pink trails down her dust-coated face.

'It was a Vour,' she murmured. '*Now* I understand what she was talking about.'

'What do you mean?' asked Aaron.

'Give me the book.'

Aaron pulled his copy of *The Devouring* from the backpack at his feet and handed it to her. She paged through it until she found what she was looking for.

'*I stayed with it for fifty years,*' Reggie read aloud. '*When the cancer began to eat at the body and it couldn't get out of bed, I knew what I was going to do. My brother would have his revenge, even if I had to do it for him. And the more bitter the wound, the sweeter the vengeance.*'

Reggie caught Eben's eyes in the rear-view mirror.

'Macie built that room and sealed Jeremiah in. She trapped the Vour when her brother died.' She closed the book. 'It's true. It's all true. Eben, what do we do?'

'I don't know, Regina. I don't know.'

'We need to –'

'No! Never return to that place. No one can know of what we've seen. And God help us if that thing is ever set free.'

They rumbled over the gravel, through the woods and out onto the main road. No one said another word the whole way home.

13

Aaron wanted to hang on to his copy of the book that night, but offered to print one out for Reggie later. When Eben dropped her off at home, she raced up to the bathroom, stripped down and let the steaming water hammer at her, as if it could wash away the horrifying memories of the Vour in the basement and of Eben spewing blood.

Back in her room, she eyed the volumes on her bookshelf: the abominations of Lovecraft, the creatures of King, Stoker's seductive vampirism, Poe's deathly plots. She and her mother had read half of them together for bedtime stories, her mother's voice giving life to all of the horrible, beautiful monsters.

'I sure hope I'm not turning you into a paranoid neurotic reading you this stuff,' Mom would say, seated in the chair by Reggie's bedside.

'Don't stop now, Mom. It's getting good!'

'It doesn't scare you?'

'Well . . . a little bit.'

'Hmmm, I guess that could be a good thing.' Mom laughed. 'That you're not scared of being scared. Maybe you won't grow up to be a wuss like me.'

'You're not a wuss, Mom.'

'In some ways I am.'

'Like how?'

'Well, sometimes, when things scare me, I want to turn and run away. But not you. You get in the face of what scares you.' She poked a finger in Reggie's cheek. 'You're a little Mithridates.'

'Miss *Who*?'

'King *Mithridates*.' Mom put the book aside. 'Mithridates became a king when he was just a boy. His greatest fear was that someone would poison him to steal his throne. So he gathered up every poison that grew in the kingdom and, as the years went by, each day he ate a tiny bit of one – wolfsbane, deadly nightshade, hemlock, snake root – a different poison every day to strengthen himself against their effects. Three times in his reign traitors poisoned him, but they couldn't kill the king. In a way, he conquered his fear by making it *part of him*. Like what we do with the books.'

'Is that *true*?' Reggie had asked, wide-eyed.

Mom nodded.

'I tell the tale that I heard told. Mithridates, he died old.'

Reggie stared at the empty chair, wishing she could go back to those times, if only for a moment.

'So, Mom, got any more words of wisdom?' she asked aloud. 'Maybe something on killing Vours? If you do, feel free to call, any time.'

She got into bed, pulled the covers around her and fell asleep, wondering if she could ever do what Jeremiah's sister had done.

The Vour's words poured through her head like sewer sludge. *Let me devour your fear. Devour your fear. Devour your fear.* It was a mantra repeated in the book as well. What did it mean?

Reggie woke with a start. She wasn't sure how long she'd been asleep, but it was dark outside. Her cell phone was ringing, chirping out Carpenter's *Halloween* theme. She grabbed at it clumsily and put it to her ear.

'Hello?' she mumbled.

'Reggie?' It was Aaron's voice. 'Reggie, I just wanted to make sure you were okay.'

'Yeah, I'm just dandy.'

'I wanted to talk about something. We have proof that Vours exist now, right?'

'I'd say so,' Reggie replied. 'Or we're all suffering a group delusion.'

'I'm trying to figure out some way to come at these things. Macie's journal's got plenty of info, but she goes so wacko partway through that it gets harder and harder to make sense of her entries.'

'I've been thinking about it too. You come up with anything?'

'Well, we saw markings like the ones in the journal on the walls of the Vour's cell. On its window too. I've looked for those symbols in every book of magical weirdness I could get my hands on. Found nothing. Macie just scrawled them without any explanation. They're useless to us right now. We have to work with what we know.'

'Which isn't a lot.'

'But better than nothing. As far as we know, it's impossible to tell a normal human from a Vour-ized one just by looking at them, but there are some signs. Vours detest the cold, for example – we proved that one with Henry. When I hit him with the snowball, his skin turned black, like a severe case of frostbite.'

'And he wanted to touch fire, so they've got some fixation with heat,' said Reggie.

'Also, we know Vours manifest as smoke. And lastly, according to Macie, Vours can't cry.'

'But how can I *stop* one?'

'That's the thing. There's no real *science* to guide us here – and we know Macie never discovered a magic bullet. If she had, she would've saved Jeremiah instead of watching him die.'

'So Henry's lost to us forever?' Reggie's voice cracked when she spoke.

'Look, we can't give up. We just can't. I have an idea,' Aaron said. 'I know this is going to sound dumb, but it's all we've got, so hear me out.'

'Okay.'

'First of all, we know they've got a weakness – the cold thing. They're not some sort of Lovecraftian Elder Gods or anything.'

'Wonderful. So I don't have to worry about Henry swallowing our entire planet. He'll just kill off pets and give me hallucinations, until he goes psycho like Joseph Garney and wipes out a Sunday school class. I'll sleep much better now.'

'Look, I'm going somewhere with this. If it has a weakness, then it's not invulnerable. If it's not invulnerable –'

'Then we can destroy it,' Reggie finished.

'Exactly.'

'So we freeze the Vour to death?' Reggie asked.

'It might not be that simple. We don't know where Henry's *consciousness* is, so killing the Vour may not be enough. You have to rescue Henry's soul, or whatever, and get it back in his body.'

'And if we freeze Henry's body, we might kill the Vour, but we'd also kill Henry.'

'There's something else,' said Aaron. 'Think about Jeremiah. His body was dead, but the Vour wasn't. It was trapped, and it couldn't get back to where it came from, but it didn't die.'

'Great. They're immortal.'

'Maybe. But right now we just have to take care of Henry, which means really going toe-to-toe with his Vour and dragging it out of his body. And that brings me to my second point,' he said. 'We know we can't fight the Vour physically, because we risk hurting Henry's body.'

'So what does that leave us?'

'There's only one thing I can think of. We need to go after them the same way they come after us. It's not our bodies they attack, for the most part. They go after our minds. What we need is a way to connect to the Vour *psychically*.'

'How are we supposed to do that?'

'That's the big question – and I don't know the answer yet.'

'You don't know? That's not much of a second point, Aaron.'

'It's still a developing plan, okay? Listen, the reason I mentioned point number two is that it leads up to point number three. If and when we get that psychic connection with the Vour, I think it's a pretty good bet it'll throw everything it's got at us. Now, what do you think is its greatest weapon?'

'Fear,' Reggie said. 'They're drawn to it. They feed on it. They attack us with it.'

'That's what I think too. Which means we've got to get a whole lot braver . . . and quickly.' Aaron chuckled bitterly.

Reggie heard voices through the vent in the wall. Dad was in Henry's room, tucking him in for the night.

'Fear is poison,' she said.

'What?'

'Fear. It's like poison,' she said, 'or a disease. You just need to build up immunity, little by little, or get an innoculation. You have to face it, and beat it, if you ever want to be able to keep it out for good.'

'Well, I don't know about you, but I've read more horror novels and seen more monster movies than anyone I know, except maybe you. And all this still scares the shit out of me. This is real.'

'I know,' she whispered. 'I've got to go. Let's talk more tomorrow.'

'Hey, Reg?'

'Yeah?'

Aaron was silent for a moment before he asked, 'Where do you think they come from? And why do they want to do this to us?'

'I'm not sure I even want to know. I just want Henry back.' She clicked off the phone.

Dad's muffled voice drifted through the vent, speaking to the thing that pretended to be Henry in the room next door. She knew what it was. It was a Vour. She knew the horror of what it could do to her, and to the people she loved. It wasn't fear she felt now – it was rage.

'*I tell the tale that I heard told*,' she said through gritted teeth, '*Mithridates, he died old*.'

Reggie climbed onto her desk chair and pressed her ear to the vent. Voices wafted in on the warm caress of central heating.

'You feeling okay?' Dad asked.

'Sorta, yeah, I guess,' said Henry.

'Sorta, yeah, I guess,' echoed Dad. 'What does that mean?'

'Well,' Henry said, 'it's Reggie.'

'What about Reggie?'

'I'm not tattling – I love Reggie. But she's different.'

Reggie's brow rose. The monster was really good. Right down to the little catch in his throat when he said, 'I love Reggie.'

'Different how?'

'I think maybe she's getting *high*, Dad,' Henry said. 'Maybe Aaron too.'

Reggie would have laughed at the thought of Aaron Cole riding around on his ten-speed with a big joint hanging out of his mouth, if the Vour hadn't been playing to Dad so well. He was better than really good. He was brilliant.

'Why would you think that?' Dad asked.

'They talked about it in school, and I saw those commercials – but, well, she's been getting weirder, and that's what they say to look for. We could make a whole list of stuff about her – right?'

Reggie heard Dad's weary sigh, and knew Henry had sunk the hook in nicely.

'Thanks for caring, Henry,' Dad said. 'Your sister's lucky to have you. Go to sleep now.'

'Okay.'

The vent's warm air bathed Reggie's cheek with a faint *whoosh*. What was Dad doing now? Kissing Henry goodnight? Pulling the covers up? Going down the hall to make a phone call to some tough-love intervention group? *Hello. My name is Thom Halloway. I have a fifteen-year-old daughter named Regina who appears to be in some sort of crisis and may be using drugs, but her mother walked out on us and I am totally incapable of functioning as a father on any meaningful, emotional level. Can you people do it for me?*

The air from the vent stopped blowing.

A whisper crept into her ear from just behind the vent. Deep. Sonorous. Frigid.

'Regina . . .'

It was Henry. Gone was the naive eight-year-old voice he'd just used with her father. The thin metal bars of the vent seemed an appropriate mouth for this voice: heartless, cold and cruel.

'You're a very curious girl,' said Henry.

'What do you mean?'

'You know what I mean, Regina. What's the old saying? Ah, I remember now. "Curiosity flayed the cat alive, ripped it apart limb from limb and listened to it scream before it killed it." That's the one.'

'Yeah.' Reggie ground her teeth. 'One of my favourites.'

'Terrified of little spiders. Poor girl. You don't stand a chance against us.'

'We'll destroy you.'

'No. You'll go mad,' it said. 'Your fear will consume you, blurring what is real and what is dream.' The voice was changing, deepening by almost imperceptible degrees of pitch – but changing just the same. 'The spiders in your room? That was just a *taste*, Regina. A *coming attraction*. You don't need your scary stories and your horror movies any more. We're going to give you the *real thing* every day of your miserable life until you lose your mind, or until your heart gives out, like that hag you left to watch over me. But I do hope you live a long, long time. Give us years to devour you from the inside out.'

'I'll stuff you back into the hole you crawled out of. I'm going to bring Henry back.'

'Don't you get it yet? I *am* Henry. The only one this world will ever know.'

A laugh echoed through the vent, shrill and ugly.

Reggie felt murderous. And, worse, she felt helpless.

The thing that used to be her brother yawned.

'Nighty night, Reg.'

But Reggie did not sleep.

You know where you need to go. What you need to do.

The clock read 2:17 when she climbed out of bed. She grabbed some supplies and a set of keys and then sneaked out of the house. She took the beat-up pickup Dad used for construction work and was soon on the road back to Fredericks.

A learner's permit didn't technically mean she could be on the road on her own, but, if she told Eben about her plan, he'd stop her. And, if she told Aaron, he'd demand to come with her. Fear had overpowered him once too often and she couldn't chance it this time.

As she drove, Reggie recalled one of Macie's journal entries: *I*

119

*know a secret now. A secret about humanity. Who has a soul and who
is a monster?*

Lost in her thoughts, she didn't see the lorry in her rear-view
mirror until it was almost on her rear bumper. Its roaring engine
made her car tremble.

'Come on, man, give me a break.'

As if it had heard her, the lorry pulled into the next lane and
sped up to pass. But when the high-mounted cab was even with
her, it slowed and kept pace.

Displaced air shoved the smaller truck left and right. Reggie
gripped the wheel until her knuckles turned white.

'What are you waiting for? Pass me!' The old pickup was like
a boat on rough seas. 'Okay, jerkoff! Fine!'

She eased her foot off the accelerator and fell back until she
was behind the lorry . . . then it slowed and fell back too. The cab
came even with her again. The lorry thundered, and the small
pickup truck shimmied closer to the icy roadside.

They had found her.

The lorry's passenger window lowered, and smoke poured
out. Blood pounded in Reggie's temples.

An old, grizzled man in a Red Sox cap and flannel coat sat
behind the wheel. His eyes locked with hers and his lips
stretched into a thin smile. He blew out a long stream of
smoke.

'Hey,' the man hollered, 'one of your tail lights is out!' He
gestured towards the back of the pickup, a smouldering cigarette
pinched between his fingers. 'Hear me? You got a busted tail
light! Drive safe now!'

He rolled up the window, shifted gears and pulled ahead.

Just a truck driver. A shepherd of the highway. Caring, thoughtful. Watching out for his fellow man. Reggie remembered something else Macie had written.

I know a secret, and secrets breed paranoia.

Once off the main road, Reggie made two wrong turns before she found the lane into the woods again. She pulled up to the house, her heartbeat thumping in her ears. Sitting there in the pickup, the little girl in her wished it all away and tried to believe it was a dream – to convince herself that if she closed her eyes she would wake up to a world where all the monsters were make-believe, and *The Devouring* was nothing more than a strange fantasy she had found in a cardboard box.

She grabbed Dad's old army duffel bag and a flashlight from the truck bed and approached the house.

Whatever the creatures were, they weren't invincible. They couldn't be. They had needs and aversions. They craved heat. They hated the cold. The Vours could interact with an organism and change its biology, enabling it to inflict horrible hallucinations but making it vulnerable to cold. This meant, according to Aaron, that they were organic, or at least physical to some degree. And, if so, then theoretically the process might work in reverse: something could interact with a Vour and change *it*. She was fuzzy on the science, if science had anything to do with it, but that didn't matter. Either Aaron was right, or she was carrying this bag for nothing, and she was dead meat.

Reggie flicked on the flashlight and stepped onto the creaky porch. Above her, the bird feeders hung motionless in the still air. She turned the knob on the front door and stepped into the dark house. The room was cold and she wanted to run.

She was going to do this – and not just for Henry. Her own fear was always awake inside her now, changing her, ruling her, *lessening* her. The Vours had more than one kind of victim. Macie was proof of that. If you *knew*, you were cursed too. Your doubt and fear would grow, obsession would take hold. She had to act now, while she still had some control. She walked across the brittle bones towards the basement hatch, her warm breath turning to mist in the freezing air. The thick darkness seemed to swallow the flashlight's narrow beam.

'*Let me out . . .*'

She threw open the trapdoor and descended.

It knew she was here. She took one of Dad's plasterboard nails from her coat pocket and clenched it, feeling the sting of the steel point.

'*Let me out . . .*'

Reggie hung one of Dad's battery-powered construction lights on the back of the chair and flipped it on. The room lit up, and through the hole Aaron had made in the wall, she could see a smoky face against the glass. The Vour had proven that it could sense her fears and send her into an alternate reality; she had to show it strength and nerve, even if it was mostly bravado.

'*I knew you'd come back.*'

The voice was sly, icy, taunting.

'You did, huh?'

'*Yes.*'

She took off her coat and put it on the chair.

'How'd you know that?'

'You all are drawn to us, as we are to you,' it said. *'For so long, I have been alone. No light, no heat . . .'*

'You had a rotting corpse. If you ask me, you got the better cell mate.'

'The last girl taunted me as well. I drove her mad.'

Macie.

'Mad, afraid, alone. You will share her fate. But I can help you. I can eat your fear. I can end your tears forever.'

'I don't want your help.'

'Lie. You want my secrets. But, if you give nothing to me, you shall take nothing from me.'

'What do you want?'

'Come closer.' A malevolent smile twisted the melting lips. *'Put your hand on the glass.'*

Reggie stepped closer and placed her fingertips on the window. The glass was so cold it burned, and its silver etchings seemed to quiver beneath her palm.

'Someone's here to see you, Regina.'

The Vour churned like boiling, muddy water, morphing into someone young and beautiful.

Her mother.

Reggie could smell the lilac lotion she dabbed on her earlobes and under her chin every morning after her shower.

They were in the bathroom. Reggie sat in a chair at the sink, looking at her mother's reflection in the cabinet mirror. Mom stood behind her, scissors in hand, giving Reggie's freshly shampooed tresses a trim.

'God, I love your hair,' Mom said. She said that every time she trimmed Reggie's hair.

'Of course you do. It's yours.'

'Regina,' Mom said, 'would you hate me if I just disappeared from your life?'

'Why would you disappear?'

'Would you rather think that I was abducted and brutally murdered, or that I just walked out because I didn't love you?'

Snip.

'The first one,' said Reggie. 'Murdered.'

'Really?' Mom said.

Snip, snip.

'I wouldn't want to spend the rest of my life thinking my mother didn't love me. That would really suck.'

'I see,' said Mom, and she stopped snipping. 'So, rather than finding a joyful life elsewhere, you'd prefer my life just ended. Violently.'

Snip.

'Well, I didn't mean –'

'If I found love somewhere else, you'd want me murdered before you'd let me have it. Isn't that right?'

Snip. Snip.

'No, that's not what –'

'It's always about *you*, isn't it?'

'Huh?'

'I brought you into the world, gave you everything I could . . . but it wasn't enough.'

She snipped again. Faster.

'Mom?'

124

'It's *never* enough – you suck the life out of me until I'm an empty shell.'

The scissor blades snapped open and shut, open and shut, and more and more of Reggie's beautiful hair fell to the floor.

'Mom, my hair! Don't –'

She tried to stand but her mother shoved her back down. The hand on Reggie's shoulder wrinkled, the fingernails split and yellowed. Her mother grew haggard and filthy.

'Look what you've done to me! Leech! Parasite!' her mother shrieked. 'What more do you want from me?'

The scissors were ravenous now, chopping off big chunks right down to the scalp, leaving mean, bare patches of skin across Reggie's skull. Mom's face knotted with anger.

'Mom, stop! Please don't –'

'What more do you want, Regina? *Blood?*'

Mom raised the scissors high. They flashed in the light like a silver-winged bird, and then she plunged them into her own wrist. She offered her arm to Reggie like a bloody sacrifice.

Reggie screamed and pulled away from the glass. She opened her balled fist. The nail had pierced her palm. The pain had broken off the hallucination. It bled and hurt like hell, but she'd stopped the nightmare.

'*You should have stayed longer. You missed the best part.*'

'I hate you,' she hissed.

The Vour grinned.

'*We can always count on people to hate and to fear. To harm one another and to be harmed. To kill and to be killed. It is what opens the gate.*'

'Yeah, sure.' Reggie snorted. 'Too bad you can't open that window, though.' Now it was Reggie who was grinning. She tapped on the glass. 'So tell me . . . can you things *die*? I'm kind of hoping you guys are immortal. Forever is a real long time to be stuck in there.'

The Vour sped at the glass. Reggie tried not to flinch.

'LET ME OUT!'

On impact, a million specks of smoke flew apart and then drifted back together like mercury. The face remade itself.

'I have to tell you,' Reggie said, 'the smash-against-the-window thing is only scary so many times. You are *never* getting out – that is, unless I say so.'

Part of her wanted to run; part of her relished the chance to study it. It exuded a foulness that was the opposite of warmth, light, goodness, love.

'Unless you say so?' it asked.

Reggie nodded.

The Vour stared back at her. This close, it still made her quake. She worked the nail into her palm until the pain took the edge off her fear. She could feel the blood warm against her skin.

'You want out? Give me back my brother.'

'We're making deals now, are we?'

'I want Henry back. When he's free, I'll set you free. That's all I care about. Make it happen.'

The black shape came still closer.

'Stupid girl. Do you think we are all of one mind, that I, one measly being, have such power? Don't you think I would have called another to free me if I was able?' It loosed a low, distorted chuckle. *'You know nothing of what we are. You confuse the servant for the master. In time, you too shall succumb to the Devouring.'*

'Oh really? How do you plan to do that? Have my eight-year-old brother torment me with magic tricks, or will you just bore me to death from inside your little cage?'

'*Perhaps you were followed. Perhaps you have enemies in your midst. Who can say?*'

The vapourous face pulsed hypnotically.

'*I have a deal for you,*' it said. '*Why don't you help me come out of here . . . and come into you? I gain freedom, you lose fear.*'

'You offered Macie the same deal, didn't you? After you lost your home inside her brother. What makes you think I would accept when she didn't?'

'*You're full of fear, Regina. In every corner of your mind. And now there is Henry. And us. So much to be afraid of. Can you imagine what your life would be like without fear?*'

Reggie's body felt rubbery; the construction light was too bright, and the room was freezing. Her hand throbbed.

'But it's not Sorry Night,' she said. 'How can you take me if it isn't Sorry Night?'

'*The solstice allows us to enter and feed upon the fearful, as I did to the boy in the cornfield.*'

The creature swirled through the corpse's remains and then slithered back out. Reggie stared at the pile of bones.

'Jeremiah,' she said. 'His name was Jeremiah.'

'*He was devoured in the dark; the light of a single flame led us to him in the midwinter night. But there is another way.*' The Vour's grin was almost lustful. '*Surrender to your fear so you may triumph over it. Choose me, open your soul to me and embrace the Devouring.*'

'Why would I do that to myself?'

The Vour pressed against the glass once more.

'*You're drawn to me as I am to you. Your weakness is my strength. Imagine the liberation, Regina.*' The voice was serene.

'But you're not human.'

'*We become human.*'

'No you don't. You're . . . a cancer,' said Reggie.

'*No. Fear is the cancer. We are the cure.*'

She heard the voice echo, and she could feel herself falling like Alice down the rabbit hole. 'What . . . are . . . you?'

'*I am beyond your understanding.*'

The Vour's eyes dissolved into the churning darkness, then returned again. She tightened her fist. The pain was excruciating.

'*If you refuse, your terror will grow worse, like the girl before you. We will hunt you. We will torture you. And we will never stop.*'

Her father appeared before her, gazing down at a photograph of her mother. With his other hand he raised a revolver and put the barrel in his mouth. His finger tightened on the trigger.

She dug the nail deep into her flesh.

'*Stop it!*' she cried.

The phantasm dissipated like smoke in the wind. The Vour rolled against the glass.

Reggie bent down and picked up the bat Aaron had dropped the day before.

'I'm scared,' she said.

The Vour smiled.

'*Good. I need you to be scared. Very, very scared. And then you'll never be scared again.*'

Reggie raised the bat; as she swung, time seemed to slow, then wood met glass, and the window shattered.

The Vour billowed, black steam gathering itself, floating before her, growing larger and denser.

'*Freedom!*'

In the bright light, the smoke shimmered; it devoured any trace of warmth around it. The basement's temperature plummeted. Reggie's breath steamed as she shivered and faced the monster.

'*Give in to your fear, Regina. Let it call to me. Surrender for me, for Henry, for all of us.*'

She nodded, but she knew that Henry wasn't an 'us'. It looked like Henry, it retained his memories – but it wasn't her brother.

The Vour whirled about. Reggie's pulse raced with adrenaline.

'Was *he* as scared as I am?' she asked, glancing at Jeremiah's bones.

'*He was easy. He wasn't as strong as you.*'

The whirlwind turned faster.

'Is it true that Vours can't cry?'

'*Yes, but you won't miss it.*'

It glided towards her.

'When it's done, what happens to the me that was scared? Does it die?'

'*It does not die.*'

'Then where does it go?'

'*To a place where it belongs, a place where it is needed.*' The Vour, a roiling cloud with a wickedly shifting face, stared at her with gleaming black eyes. '*It is time. I can feel it in you. I can hear it. Let your fear take you over, so you may say goodbye to it forever.*' The voice was a seductive whisper.

She whispered back. 'Tell me why you hate the cold.'

'*Because without you, it's all we can ever feel.*'

'Well, if you hate the cold,' she said, 'then I've got a surprise for you.'

Reggie whipped a fire extinguisher out of the duffel bag.

'This is for Henry!'

She pulled the pin and fired, and with a loud whoosh a frigid white cloud of CO_2 jetted into the Vour. The thing howled and thrashed. Reggie fired another blast, holding down the trigger until a haze of CO_2 obscured everything. The swirling smoke slowed, and the monster's moans faded until everything was silent and still. Reggie dropped the extinguisher.

'Cold enough for you? Huh?'

White mist sparkled like fairytale snow. In the fog, Reggie saw something on the ground. She carefully crept towards it, fanning the cloud away.

It was an abomination unlike any she could've imagined. The thing lay on the floor like a prehistoric fish. It had the semblance of an elongated human torso, but rather than legs the body tapered down into a fleshy tail. In place of arms, several slimy tentacles protruded from its sides and lay in tangled piles all around it. It had no visible eyes or ears, and where it seemed a head might have been, there was instead a giant round mouth with an iridescent tongue lolling out between rings of black teeth. Lumps and veins covered its oily skin. It reeked like rotting leaves.

All of the adrenaline and tension drained from Reggie's body, and she started to weep. Her shoulders shook with every sob. She'd done it. She'd destroyed a Vour.

But, in the harsh light, the frozen hide began to sweat beads of pale green liquid. Yellow sludge bubbled up from the mouth and pooled on the floor. The remains of the monster sagged and oozed into a pool, like toxic waste, nearing Reggie's boots. It touched the soles and climbed onto the scuffed leather. Reggie's stomach twisted. The Vour wasn't disintegrating – it was changing. The lumps of its broken body morphed into dozens of new creatures.

Blood-red spiders.

They leaped at Reggie's feet, and she swatted and stomped furiously, determined to crush every last one. The spiders burst beneath her boots like pustules until the floor glistened with their crushed remains. Out of the corner of her eye, Reggie saw something scuttle across the floor, a small puff of black smoke spilling from a red abdomen.

The Vour's voice echoed in her head. *Fear is the cancer. We are the cure.*

Reggie snatched up the spider. It stared at her, eyes filled with hate.

Fear is the cancer. We are the cure.

The story of King Mithridates. Eat the poison. Make it a part of yourself.

She grabbed the spider with both hands. It wriggled in her grasp. *We are the cure.* Her jaw hurt from gritting her teeth. *We devour your fear.* She brought the spider to her mouth.

Devour your fear.

She opened her mouth and stuffed in the horror. Its fangs dug into her tongue, a hot, searing pain. The hairy legs flailed against the inside of her cheeks. The spider belly squirmed against her throat. She gagged, and the spider wiggled halfway out, but she crammed it back in and bit down.

The tough flesh of the spider's abdomen burst between her molars, filling her mouth and throat with a gush of thick, bitter liquid. She growled, forcing herself to bite down again and again. The meaty fang-appendages squashed between her front teeth. Her brain screamed: *Devour your fear!* She gagged again but kept chewing; she turned the spider to a slick, bristly mash. Nausea surged from her stomach, but she sucked in as much air as she could through her nose and swallowed. The vileness slid down her throat, still twitching.

A final gulp and it was done.

She slumped, gasping, spitting, shivering from the cold but drenched in sweat. The lump of Vour remains was gone. The thing was inside her now, in her blood. The monster had not taken her over. She had enslaved the monster.

'*You will regret doing that,*' it said in her mind.

Reggie grinned weakly.

'I already do,' she said. 'You taste like ass.'

Then Reggie sank against the wall, into oblivion.

———

Reggie awoke on the basement floor. Something was leaking through the ceiling boards. She caught a drop of the liquid in her hand and sniffed it.

Gasoline.

Footsteps crunched on the bones above. Someone else was in the house. Reggie raced up the steps and pushed against the trapdoor. It wouldn't budge. Heat radiated from the ceiling.

She put her shoulder to the door and shoved as hard as she

could. The trapdoor opened a couple of centimetres, and the heat and light of flames lashed at her face before it fell again.

'Come on!'

She threw herself against the door. It lurched open and fire roared all around. Thick swirling smoke choked and blinded her. Reggie staggered backwards, tumbled down the cellar stairs, and hit the dirt floor.

She lay on her stomach, coughing and wheezing. Her clothes were smoking and she smelled her singed hair. She staggered up, and ash floated down around her. The stairs caught fire and blazed as she circled, looking for options. She dragged the chair across the floor and set it beneath one of the basement's high windows, then stepped on it and stretched up on her tiptoes.

She jumped, but her fingertips were still half a metre away from the window. The ceiling had become a sheet of fire, and the smoke and heat were suffocating. She grabbed the empty fire extinguisher and hurled it through the window, and the hot air sucked out of the room.

She'd bought herself a little more time.

With a sudden, torturous *crack*, the stairs collapsed into the room. The flames pushed Reggie back, roaring like demons, hemming her in.

She looked up and saw a cast-iron pipe a metre below the ceiling that ran the length of the room. The house wasn't straight, and neither was the pipe. It was lower at one end of the room than the other, and it rose up all the way to the window.

Reggie set the chair against the far wall, squatted and sucked cooler air near the floor deep into her lungs. She climbed onto the chair and jumped. Her hands grasped the pipe, the metal already hot enough to sear her palms. She moaned but would not let go.

Ignore the pain. Let go and you burn to death.

A metre above the pipe, the fire licked the ceiling. Her flesh stuck to the hot pipe. The blood on her pierced palm sizzled.

Keep going. Focus on the window.

Hand over hand, inch by inch. Three metres to go. Two and a half.

There was a sudden, sharp creak and the pipe sagged behind her. Its iron was giving out. Two metres. One and a half. The pipe groaned again and snapped behind her. Her end of it swung towards the window, and Reggie lunged. Her burned fingers snagged the window frame as the rest of her slammed into the wall.

She hung there, heaving, desperate for air.

Do a pull-up, or die.

Reggie pulled her aching body up and through the window as the ceiling caved in behind her.

She fell into the backyard and crawled across the icy lawn. She collapsed and let the frost bathe her cheek. Crisp, early morning air slid down her throat. She pressed her blistered fingers into the cold earth.

She looked back at the house through blurry, tear-filled eyes. The entire thing was a ball of fire. On the other side of the house, an engine revved, tyres screeched and the car of her would-be killer peeled away.

———

The drive home was filled with visions of spiders, shadowy monsters and the cold eyes of the thing that lived inside her brother's body. Only the sickening ache in her hands kept Reggie grounded enough to keep from swerving off the icy road. She skidded to a stop in her driveway and staggered out of the car. The sun was just peeking out over the horizon.

At the front door, her burned hands shook so much, the key kept missing the lock, and she dropped it on the stoop. She reached down to grab it and, when she straightened up, Henry stood in front of her. He was barefoot in his Spider-Man pyjamas, grinning, and he held a piece of muffin.

'Blueberry. Last one.' He popped it in his mouth. 'Show and tell,' he said, opening his mouth wide to display the chewy glop. Reggie thought of the twisted, grotesque torso on the basement floor, the yellow slime bubbling out of its maw.

'Bad hair day, sis. So, where you been?'

'Destroying one of your wicked little buddies.'

Henry's eyes turned to slits. 'You're lying.'

'You're right. I didn't just destroy it. I busted it into a million frozen pieces. And then I *ate* it.'

The boy stepped back and Reggie stalked him into the foyer.

'Scared? Not me. Not any more. I devoured my fear, you little freak. What do you think about that?' She shoved Henry hard in the chest and he fell to the floor. 'And now I'm coming after you. I'm getting my brother back.'

'Henry belongs to me now,' the boy seethed as he scuttled away. 'You can't get him back.'

'No?' Reggie towered over him now. 'Then maybe I'll start kicking your ass until you'd rather be somewhere else.'

She loved her brother, but he was somewhere beyond her reach, and a body without a soul was just fibres and fluids. She grabbed him by the shirt, yanked him out of the front door and threw him onto the snowy lawn.

'Dad!' The boy looked up at the second-floor windows.

Reggie placed a foot on his chest and he sprawled out in the snow.

'Dad! Help me!' He sounded so real, so like Henry.

Reggie slapped him hard across the face. His hand flew to his cheek. He shivered in the snow as black veins spread across his bare feet and up his ankles.

'Cold.' He rattled. 'Too cold.'

'What's the matter, Henry?' Reggie dug a knee into his stomach. 'You love the snow.'

'Let me up!'

The cold turned him a greyish blue. He writhed in agony and tried to rise, but Reggie grabbed his wrists and shoved him back down. The Vour roiled beneath the skin as the monster seethed inside the boy's body.

Reggie squeezed Henry's wrists harder, forcing them deeper into the snow. He squealed and she felt something awaken in her and race through her veins.

A door opened deep in her mind.

'How . . .' the Vour croaked.

The fabric of reality tore around her; the warp and weave of time and space contorted and collapsed. Reggie couldn't tell where her body started and Henry's ended. The world of Cutter's Wedge melted away as she fell through an invisible psychic barrier and into a cold, black abyss . . .

14

Darkness receded from the edges of her vision like a slow tide.

She lay in a thick, wet fog. Through the mist she heard laughter, the grinding of calliope music, and the *ding-ding-ding*s of carnival games. She perceived the faint aromas of caramel and buttered popcorn. Confused, she stumbled towards the sounds and smells. She had just been out on her frozen lawn fighting with the monster inside Henry. Where was she now?

The fog parted, and the mud beneath Reggie's feet gave way to sawdust. Game booths, candy-floss vendors and balloon-toting clowns filled a crowded walkway. A roller-coaster, a log ride, a fun house and an enormous Ferris wheel punctuated the dark sky. Reggie pushed through a red turnstile and walked into a dreamlike version of the Bottle Hill fairgrounds.

Gaggles of happy children ran from one booth to the next, carrying doughnuts and stems of candy floss, and one tiny girl skipped by with a bear almost twice her size. As she passed Reggie, the girl tripped and fell on her plushy prize. Reggie reached down to help her, but the girl popped up on her own and raced after her friends, laughing.

Since she was four, Reggie and her parents had driven each

summer to the town of Bottle Hill for its annual four-day carnival. The first three years it had just been Reggie. The summer after Henry was born, Reggie and Dad rode the Ferris wheel again and again, waving down from the top at Mom and the blue stroller far below.

The carnival, more than any other place, reminded Reggie of the happy times her family once shared. Even when she had outgrown the joys of roller-coasters and bumper cars, Reggie took vicarious delight in watching Henry. He loved the Bottle Hill Festival as much as she had.

Until Mom left. They had not been back since.

With every passing moment, the scents grew richer, the noises louder, the colours brighter. The memory of the fight with Henry pulsed like a failing heartbeat in the back of her mind. She tried to revive it, to resuscitate the details – the snow, the cold, the smoke in the boy's eyes. But the memory faded beneath the sounds, smells and sights of the carnival.

She stood in front of the Ferris wheel and looked up. The red, yellow and white carriages swung in the breeze as the ride slowed and stopped. A freckled red-haired boy and an apple-cheeked blonde girl hopped out of a carriage and scampered down the ramp, clutching strips of pink ride tickets and ice-cream cones. The little girl dragged a teddy bear behind her.

'Hey!' Reggie shouted. Her voice sounded paper-thin.

The boy stopped and gave her a puzzled look.

'Who are you?' he asked.

Reggie moved towards him, but the boy stepped back.

'You're a stranger here,' he said. The boy took a lick of chocolate-chip ice cream.

138

'An intruder,' added the little girl.

'An intruder where?' Reggie clutched the boy's shoulders. 'Where are we?'

The blonde girl glared at her. She whispered in her teddy bear's ear and then held it up in front of Reggie. It looked mangy and dirty, and its eyes were missing.

'I can see you,' said the girl, wagging the bear at Reggie.

Black smoke poured from the bear's eye sockets. A glistening tongue shot out of its mouth and waggled at Reggie. She stumbled backwards and let out a startled cry. The girl giggled and raced off.

'Where am I?'

The boy opened his mouth to speak, but he only made guttural clacking sounds.

His tongue had been sliced off.

Blood oozed from the stump and coated his teeth. He dropped his cone and ran after the girl. Reggie stood there, shocked. The ice cream pulsated and oozed in the sawdust at her feet. It formed a crude face, the cone sitting atop its head like a crooked dunce cap. The face gurgled at her in a high voice:

> *You've been devoured by his fear,*
> *And he will spend forever here!*

Reggie picked up the cone.

'Whose fear? Devoured by whose fear?'

The ice cream dripped from her hand to the ground.

A wave of children ran past Reggie towards a bustling game stall, and Reggie followed, peering over the dozen little bobbing heads. Three water guns were bolted to the middle of a splintery wooden counter, and ratty stuffed animals hung from rusted nails around the booth.

Reggie knew the game well. Be the fastest kid to shoot water into your plastic clown's mouth, pop the balloon behind its head and win a prize. This was how Henry had won Kappy, his beloved koala. Mom had been so proud.

'Where are the heads?' asked a curly haired boy, hopping up and down.

'Here they come!' shouted a boy with thick glasses and a baseball cap. 'Look! Here come the heads! Here come the heads!' He pointed to a tall, thin clown in a brown-stained polka-dot jumpsuit who had stepped out from behind a curtain.

The clown had one hand tucked inside his suit, and the other held the decapitated heads of three children by the hair. Their expressions were a mix of shock and fright. The scene was like something torn from a B-horror movie, but that did not reassure Reggie. Beneath the scent of butter and cotton candy lay the rankness of death and decay.

The clown put the severed heads in a row on a table, and two girls stepped onto the rickety milk crates set in front of the counter. The excited crowd pushed a little boy up onto a third crate between them. Both girls turned to the boy and giggled, wispy black smoke curling out of their eye sockets. They pressed their smoky eyes against the scopes and wrapped their fingers round the triggers. The boy tried to step down, but the throng forced him back up.

The boy turned his head. The curly hair, the round face, the wide and terrified eyes . . .

'Henry!' Reggie screamed, but her voice was drowned by the loud blare of the clown's air horn. 'Henry, it's me!' Reggie pushed forward, but the cheering kids blocked her. Dozens of black eyes oozed smoke as the crowd's excitement grew.

'Stay away from him!' she yelled.

A pug-nosed boy punched her in the gut. Reggie choked at the blow and hunched over her stomach, coughing and gasping for breath. She crawled through the sawdust, the demented children kicking and shoving her down every time she tried to rise to her feet.

'Please . . .' Reggie burbled. 'Don't hurt my brother . . .'

She looked over the crowd to see the girls firing bursts of red fluid from their pistols. The brains expanded out from the top of the heads like balloons.

Henry placed his trembling hands on the pistol in front of him and squeezed. The red stream shot into the air and drenched a prize, a one-eyed toy monkey, dangling from a beam.

The crowd erupted in laughter.

Reggie staggered to her feet, her legs still shaking from the blow. She pushed a little girl aside and attempted to reach Henry again. The girl snapped her head towards Reggie.

'Look! I got my face painted!' Her cheeks morphed into a squirming palette of bugs and slimy larvae, hanging raggedly from her jaws. 'Do you like it?' Thick segmented worms writhed out from her face and crawled onto Reggie's arms. 'Want me to paint yours?'

Reggie recoiled and slapped at the worms. They turned to black smoke and left a powdery residue on her skin.

Henry slipped from his crate and fell backwards into the

141

sawdust. His gun spurted into the tattered awning of the booth. Laughter boomed again and one of the kids kicked the fallen boy.

The brains of the girls' targets stretched to maximum capacity, quavered for a moment from the pressure and then exploded simultaneously with sickening *pop*s, splattering the clown's costume. He sounded the air horn several times, then turned his eyes on Henry. The ghoulish children backed away and taunted the boy as he scrambled to his feet.

'You lost, scaredy cat!'

'Better run!'

'Better hide!'

'Better keep your brains inside!'

Reggie called out to her brother, but he couldn't hear her over the jeers. The crowd held her back with chilled hands as the clown hopped onto the booth counter. Smiling madly, he pulled his hidden arm from inside his costume. Fused to his wrist where his hand should have been was a rusty, bloodstained hatchet.

'Henry!' Reggie cried. 'Run!'

Her brother's screams echoed through the carnival. He scampered towards the walkway, the clown skipping behind him in his floppy shoes, honking his air horn and swinging his axe hand.

Reggie wrenched free of the laughing children and ran after her brother and the killer clown, but lost track of them near the Ferris wheel. Close by, a rusty dunk tank brimmed with churning red gore. Submerged in that sludge of entrails, a vaguely human shape writhed. Reggie backed away.

She circled the roller-coaster tracks and raced past the concession stands. Human torsos, headless and limbless, lay on the food counters. They'd been gutted with ribs splayed wide. Chest cavities had been filled with crushed ice and chilled bottles of dark liquid. Unspeakable dismemberments sizzled on greasy grills, emitting a fleshy burning scent that soured in her mouth. Plastic log cars whooshed down the flume ride, splashing into a pool choked with bloated corpses.

There was no trace of her brother or the clown.

She raced by a whirling carousel. Gone were the white horses and unicorns from childhood memory, replaced by black-horned demons and grey sharp-winged gargoyles. Reggie looked around in desperation.

'Henry!' she screamed. 'Henry, where are you?'

The clown's air horn blared in the distance. Reggie jumped aboard the carousel and raced across to the other side just in time to see the clown disappear through the swirling, striped cylinder at the fun-house entrance.

She followed, tripping and stumbling through the spinning tube, and finally fell into the Hall of Mirrors. Here she was surrounded by distortions of her own image: short and squashed; tall, rail thin and pointy-headed; a wavy corkscrew; puckered eyes, lips and ears. The floor and ceiling were mirrored too. Everything moved, twisted, and undulated. Bile crept up Reggie's throat, but she continued to stumble through the maze, bumping into the walls, calling for Henry.

But as she progressed through the labyrinth, her reflections turned into Henry in different stages of life. Here, he was a boy of five, crying for the loss of his grandmother; there, an old man, cancerous and brittle, as their grandfather had been for months before he died.

She whirled round and saw the reflection of a small skeleton.

'Not real, Reggie. None of this can be *real*.' The visions melted away and Reggie's image now stared back at her. She leaned against a mirror and closed her eyes, listening. The maze was silent save the sound of her ragged breathing.

'Please, Henry,' she whispered. 'Answer me.'

Something shuffled across the floor. In the mirrors, clown shoes spread out in both directions, splattered with blood. Reggie looked up to see an infinite line of rusty axe blades raised above her head. She ducked as the hatchets fell.

One sliced into her right shoulder.

The blade tore through her shirt and into her flesh. Reggie screamed as blood spattered onto the mirrored glass wall. She scrambled deeper into the labyrinth, smacking into mirrors and staggering down the corridors. Soon her legs became leaden and her motions slow, as if all of time was grinding to a halt around her. Sound and colour faded from the world.

Her surroundings became translucent, like glass sculptures set against churning darkness, and then they faded away. Paralysed, she tumbled through a void, helpless and without light, warmth or hope . . .

———

Something cool touched Reggie's skin. She opened her eyes; snowflakes fell on her nose and lashes. The carnival was gone – the ghastly children, the mirrors, the clown. Gone.

She was on her lawn again. Next to her lay Henry, only semi-conscious. He moaned and gasped with his eyes closed.

'Out,' he whispered. 'Get out!'

Then the boy bolted upright in the snow, his eyes wide in fright. He ran his trembling fingers over his face as if to make sure he was alive. Then he pounced like a feral cat on Reggie, who was too confused to react, too weak to fight him off.

'How did you do that?' the boy spat. His fingers tightened around her throat. 'I'll rip your head off for that!'

A snow shovel slammed across Henry's back and knocked him to the ground.

'You touch her again and I'll rip *your* head off.' Aaron pulled Reggie to her feet. 'Get out of here, you evil little bastard.'

'You'll pay,' said Henry, rising to his feet. Smoke wisped around his cold eyes. 'You should never have entered our domain. We'll come for you now. Both of you.'

The boy stumbled inside and slammed the front door. The deadbolt clicked.

'*Domain?*' Aaron asked as he helped his weakened friend to her feet. 'Reggie, just where the hell did you go?'

15

Reggie sat on Aaron's bed while he knelt in front of her and bandaged her hands. Horror-movie posters covered the walls. All the mask-wearing slashers, bloodthirsty demons and ravenous undead they depicted seemed more comforting than scary. They were familiar icons from the times when fear had been a game. Those times were over.

She felt as if she'd been mashed into scrap by an industrial crusher. She was coated with ash, and her burned hair was a wild mess. The one thing she found pretty about herself she'd have to cut off. Aaron had given her a black knit hat to cover it up, at least. She'd told him the whole story of what had happened as he went about tending to her injuries. So far, he'd said nothing in response.

'Say something,' she said.

He raised his head, his look a mix of worry and anger.

'What do you want me to say, Reg? That I'm cool with the fact you went back without me? That you faced that thing alone?'

'Aaron, I –'

'You could have *died* in that fire.' Aaron taped the ends of the gauze on both hands and turned her palms upwards tenderly. 'You're lucky the rest of your body isn't like this.'

Reggie cradled her arms to her chest. 'I know, but –'

'And eating that thing!' Aaron stood up and paced. 'Do you have any idea what kind of toxin you might have ingested? Who knows what their physical composition is? Plus, the mental damage you could've –'

'Henry's my brother, Aaron. You said we had to get braver. So I did.'

'Reg, I – I know I freaked out when we saw the Vour. But it won't happen again. I won't let you down a second time.'

Reggie rose from the bed and hugged him.

'I know. And that's why I need you. You've got to help me figure this out.' She gestured at his computer workstation.

Aaron grinned. 'Now that I can help with.'

He swept a pile of soda cans off his desk and sat down at his computer. Reggie took stock of Aaron's bedroom. As usual, it was a mess: empty cans of hyper-caffeinated energy drinks littered the floor and adorned shelves, dressers and speakers, surrounding his collection of plastic monster figures like strange aluminum idols. Reams of scribbled notebooks towered in a pile on his nightstand, and all three computer monitors displayed peculiar web pages: the site for the Institute of Parapsychology in Boston, an amateurish alien abduction page complete with cheesy clip art of a flying saucer and animated tractor beam, and an intimidating federal government text file that nobody save Aaron would have the mental fortitude to read. In the middle of his workstation, under the light of a desk lamp, was the journal.

As Aaron worked, Reggie curled up on his bed and closed her eyes. She meant to doze for only a few minutes, but it was nearly dark when she awoke to the hissing of another can-tab snapping open.

'Thought I'd let you sleep awhile.' Aaron took a sip of his drink. 'I know you're exhausted.'

'What happened to me, Aaron?' Reggie stood up and crossed to his desk. 'Tell me you've found something to explain what's going on.'

'For starters, I think eating the Vour altered your mind.' He picked up a pencil and tapped Reggie on the head. 'You're not a Vour in there, but you're connected to them somehow. You can plug in to something or some place. Don't know what or where it is, but you went there when you latched on to Henry in the snow. So physical contact triggers it, or extreme cold, anger . . .'

'But how did I make it happen? I could feel the Vour pushing back against me. Fighting to tap into my fear.'

'The way it happened when Henry tried to drown me. Part of that monster entered my mind while it was touching me. It pushed part of itself into my brain and pulled my fears to the surface.'

'But –'

'*But* you pushed back.'

'Yeah.'

Aaron grabbed a piece of cookie from the snack bowl on the floor and popped it into his mouth.

'Listen to this.' He opened the journal to an earmarked page. 'Macie wrote this passage decades after the Vours took Jeremiah, when he was dying of cancer. I never paid attention to it until today: *Jeremiah talked in his sleep again last night. He's been doing it since the cancer started, and it breaks my heart to hear it. He sounds just like the young boy I loved, and he's crying out – "I'm so scared! Save me, Pa! Get me out of here!"*'

'It sounds like he's trapped in a nightmare,' Reggie murmured.

Aaron nodded.

'Suppose there's a place inside our heads we don't know is there. A place crammed full of such horrible stuff our mind won't even let our *subconscious* know it exists. This domain that the thing threatened you with. It's like a . . . a *fearscape*.'

Aaron turned to the Institute monitor where he pulled up a large, three-dimensional diagram of a brain. He clicked an icon on the screen and the diagram rotated, showcasing the numerous folds and intricate neural net of the model.

'You think they invade us through our brains?' asked Reggie.

'Why not? I mean, there are workings in the brain we don't have a clue about. Dark, uncharted territory. But there's *something* between Vours and humans, a synergy that allows Vours to access our fears, take over the mind and rule the body.'

Aaron double-clicked the brain schematic, and the screen magnified a small nub near the base of the model.

'This little almond-shaped thing is called the "amygdala". Part of the brain scientists isolate as the core of emotional sensation, where we experience raw, unfiltered emotion. No thinking, no intellect, just the heavy-duty stuff. Euphoria. Rage. Panic.'

'And fear.'

'Exactly.' Aaron sat back and started gnawing on a pencil. 'What if it's a door for the Vours? What if they find a way in here and *open somebody's fearscape*? Use it. Manipulate it. It's made from our own fears, and I think you were *in your own head* when you connected with that monster, Reg.'

'No. I felt it pushing me *away*. Trying to keep me *out* of somewhere. And if the fearscape is made from my fears, why a carnival? And why was Henry there?'

'The carnival's just a backdrop. Henry's the key. Right now there's nothing you're more terrified about than that Vour taking Henry.'

'But it didn't feel like *my* nightmare.' Reggie grabbed a piece of cookie. 'A killer clown in an evil carnival? Come on.'

'Don't get too concrete about this.' Aaron stood and paced his own trail. 'The mind likes *symbols*. A clown could symbolize dozens of fears.'

'Yeah, well, it felt pretty concrete.'

'I'm sure it did, but we're talking psychic trauma, not actual, physical danger.' Aaron massaged his temples. 'How'd the clown try to kill you?'

'He tried to slice me in half with his cute little hatchet-hand. Who knew my deepest fears are so damn cliché?'

'A hatchet-handed clown?'

Aaron stood up and scanned a shelf of DVDs. He pulled one out and showed it to Reggie.

'*This* hatchet-handed clown?'

The psycho clown stared back at Reggie from the DVD cover.

'That's . . . that's him,' she said.

'*Killer Karnival 2: The Return of Berzerko*. Your memory of the movie triggered the sequence! Now we're getting somewhere.'

'But I've never seen this movie.'

'You saw him in the original *KK*.'

Reggie shook her head.

'Never saw that one either.'

'Yes, you did. Henry took my copy a few months ago and said you wanted –' Aaron's jaw slackened. 'He never gave it to you.'

'No.'

'He watched it himself,' said Aaron.

Reggie sat down on the bed. 'I wasn't in *my* head, Aaron. I was in *his*.'

'Yeah, of course,' Aaron said slowly. Reggie could practically see the wheels turning in his head. 'I've been looking at it backwards. It didn't attack you. *You* attacked *it*.'

'I was mostly running in terror.'

'Maybe it felt that way. But they gain access through our minds, right? With the Vour essence inside you, you can do it too. I'll bet they were surprised as hell when you showed up. You're a freaking super-shaman!'

'I'm not a super-anything, Aaron.' Reggie glared at him. 'If I were, my brother wouldn't be trapped in a killer carnival. And there's something the Henry-Vour said that's bothering me – just the way he said that I "should never have entered *their* domain".'

'And?'

'What if the fearscape isn't in Henry's mind? What if it's in another place entirely? An actual place, like another dimension or something?'

'Then you're even more badass than I thought. You're hitting them where they come from.'

'If I didn't know better, I'd say you were *excited* about all this.'

'Damn right – don't you see, Reg? Wherever it is that Henry's at, *you can reach him.*'

Aaron clapped his hands on Reggie's shoulders. She howled in pain.

'What'd I do?' Aaron jumped back. 'More burns?'

Reggie gingerly touched her right arm.

'My shoulder . . .' She unbuttoned the top of her shirt.

Aaron moved behind her as she pulled her shirt off her shoulder. He couldn't stifle a gasp.

'Jesus,' he whispered. 'What the hell is *that*?'

Reggie looked at the wound in the mirror on the closet door. Aaron came to her side. They stared at a lesion running twenty centimetres down her back. It looked like a wound carved from *inside* her skin.

'That's where the hatchet slashed me, in the fun house,' Reggie whispered.

'I'm going to touch it, okay?' Aaron said.

'Gentle.'

Aaron put a fingertip on the wound. 'I can feel it. It's real –'

A noxious wisp of smoke seeped out of it.

'Oh, God, what's happening to me?' Reggie looked stricken.

'Wait – look!'

Slowly, the wound closed from the centre out towards the ends. Her flesh rippled beneath. The wound had healed from *underneath*.

'Unreal.'

Only the faintest black scar remained, thin as a thread, almost invisible.

'Psychic trauma, my ass. What the hell do you call *that*?'

The phone rang, making them both jump. Aaron checked the caller ID.

'Your house. Must be your dad wondering what happened. Want me to –'

'No. Let me get it.' Reggie picked up the receiver but did not speak. She could hear the boy's raspy breathing.

'Come home, Reggie.' Henry's voice sounded calm and sweet. 'I don't want to fight any more. Don't you love me?'

'You're not Henry.'

'Of course I am. I remember everything, Reggie. I remember all the times you read to me, all the scary stories –'

'You have my brother's memory, but you're not him.'

'Dad thinks so. He loves me just the way I am,' Henry said.

'I'll take you out.' Reggie's voice was low and grim. 'I swear on my life I *will* take you out.'

'Nah. You just caught me unprepared today.' Henry's sugary tone vanished. 'It won't happen again. Besides, I hate to see you upsetting Dad. You know he's a wreck since Mom left. And he looks so fragile when he's sleeping.'

Reggie went cold. 'Stay away from him.'

'Then be a good sister and come home. I'll let you read me a story. One with a happy ending.' The line clicked off, and there was only silence.

Reggie hung up the phone. She buried her face in her burned, trembling hands.

'He's going to hurt Dad if I don't go home.'

She walked to the window and stared out. Flecks of snow whipped in the air.

'I found him, Aaron. I found him in there. The real Henry. Now I need to find a way to get him out.'

'We will. You get some sleep and then –'

'Tonight. I'm going back into the fearscape tonight,' she said. 'I can't leave him in there, now that I know.'

'But look at you. I'm worried. You're a wreck.'

'Henry – the *real* Henry – has been living out his worst nightmares ever since Sorry Night.' Reggie held up her bandaged hands. 'This is nothing compared to that. We have to figure out how to beat this thing.'

Aaron nodded. 'It hates the cold. You got inside when you had it pinned in the snow. Maybe that's when their grip on the mind is weakest. We need to get it outside. Somewhere no one can see us.'

'The snow was enough to weaken it, but I got pushed out before I could find Henry. We need a real deep freeze. Like Cutter's Lake,' Reggie said. 'The water below the ice.'

'That might kill him, Reggie.'

They stared out at the mean winter landscape. Icicles gleamed like knives from the eaves. The sky hung black and cold, and the yard looked frozen and dead. Every year, winter murdered the world. What if spring never came?

'I'd rather kill him than make him live in that hell.'

'Agreed.'

'Aaron?'

'Yeah?'

'Is there an entry in the journal called "How to Find Your Brother in His Fearscape"?'

'Nope. You write that chapter yourself, baby.'

Aaron smiled at her, but Reggie could see the worry in his face.

Aaron kneaded his hands. 'There's one other thing . . .'

'What is it?' asked Reggie.

'In the fearscape, an imaginary blade cuts. And it cuts you from the inside out.'

Reggie instinctively touched her shoulder.

'Wounds in the fearscape are real,' he said. 'Not the same as in this reality, but they inflict damage. And my guess is you just got a small taste of it. If you . . . die . . . in the fearscape –'

'I could die for real.' Reggie grabbed their jackets and threw Aaron's at him. 'I understand the risk. What else can I do? I'll face it. Whatever it is. I'll get Henry out.'

Reggie ran down the stairs, and Aaron followed her out on to the driveway. When the door closed behind them, Reggie felt a grim weight gather in the pit of her stomach.

'The lake's three miles from here,' Reggie said. 'There's no way we can bike –'

'We'll take this, instead.' He pointed to his mom's hulking silver SUV. His dad's Honda looked like a Matchbox car beside it. 'She's in New York on business for the next few days.'

'Won't your dad notice it's gone?'

'Are you kidding? It's after ten o'clock. He's probably sleeping like the dead already.' Aaron blew into his hands, his fingers white from the freezing air.

'Get the keys, then. Hurry! That thing is alone in my house with my dad.'

Aaron started back in the house but then paused.

'Hypothermia and drowning are real dangers here, Reg. You need to accept that.'

'I know. But what –'

'Give me just ten minutes. Let me put together an emergency kit to warm you guys up – you know, dry blankets, warm towels. I think we have a hot-water bottle here somewhere.'

'No time. Get that kit together. Meet me at my house. I'll drag that bastard out on the lawn by his hair if I have to.'

Reggie sprinted down the driveway and into the street.

'Reggie! Wait!'

'Be there, Aaron!'

She didn't turn round.

16

The distance between the Halloways' and the Coles' was exactly three-quarters of a mile, but tonight it felt as if a small country separated the two homes. The wind slapped Reggie's face as she made her way.

Two figures leaned against a lamppost across the street, hot cherries burning at the ends of two cigarettes. Smoke streamed out of their nostrils. Black hoodies were pulled tightly around their faces. The pair looked like matching gargoyles.

The Kassner twins.

Reggie quickened her pace and avoided looking at them as she passed. The twins were the last people she wanted to come across in the dark, especially tonight. When she glanced back at the lamppost, they were gone.

Reggie sighed in relief and turned back to the sidewalk. Her heart jumped. Keech stood directly in her path now, towering over her, just a few steps away. His lips pulled back into a yellow-toothed smile and emitted a long wisp of smoke. Behind her, Mitch's boots thumped down the sidewalk, his bulk casting a long, bladelike shadow.

Fear seized Reggie as Keech reached out to grab her. She

recoiled from him and stumbled over the kerb, turning her ankle and falling into the street. Her knee scraped on the tarmac, and one of her forearms cracked hard against the road. The twins' empty eyes stared down at her from the sidewalk.

'Get the hell away from me!' she screamed, scrambling to her feet again.

A pair of headlights blinded her, and a pristine Mustang screeched to a halt. The tinted passenger-side window rolled down. Reggie stood up and sighed with relief at the sight of Quinn.

'Hey, Reggie,' he said. His smile faded when he saw Keech and Mitch.

'Guys,' Quinn said coolly.

'Yo, Cap,' Keech grumbled.

'A little far from home, aren't you?'

The twins shrugged.

Quinn reached across his seat and opened the passenger door.

'Get in, Reggie.'

Reggie slipped into the car and slammed the door shut. She looked at Keech through the window. His face was pale against the black hood. Quinn revved the engine and they sped away.

The heat in the car thawed Reggie's bones and the bitter night melted away. Despite all the turmoil, Reggie managed to relax.

'They didn't hurt you, did they?' Quinn asked, flashing Reggie a concerned look. 'I'll kick their asses if they –'

'No, no,' Reggie said hurriedly. 'I think they were just trying to scare me, and I tripped. It was stupid.'

'I just – I saw them, and you on the ground, and I thought . . .'

'I'm fine,' said Reggie. 'But you do have good timing. I'm starting to think you're my guardian angel or something.'

'Angel, huh?' He smiled.

'Here's me.' She pointed to her house, but Quinn cruised past it. 'You overshot. I live back there.'

'I just thought, well, we could take a drive,' he said. His voice was shy. 'Maybe talk a little.'

Reggie almost choked. The dashboard clock showed that she only had a few minutes to get Henry outside before Aaron showed up, and here was Quinn trying to make a move.

'Quinn, I would really love to. I'm serious. But I have to get home. My brother – he just doesn't like to be alone.'

'I won't keep you long.'

The heater blazed. Beads of sweat rose on her forehead.

'I really shouldn't. He'll get –'

'Scared? Nah. I think he's got over that.'

The neighbourhood thinned out as they headed into the countryside.

'What?' she said.

'Henry's got over *all* his fears.'

Reggie's heart quaked. Quinn's voice had changed. It was harsh now, like Henry's had been since the Vour had taken him over. Smirking, Quinn glanced over at her, and a sudden chill racked her body. The Mustang's engine roared, picking up speed. Reggie clutched the dash with her bandaged fingers.

'Oh, God. No. Please . . . not *you*.'

'Come on, Halloway. You really think a guy like me would hook up with you? A flat-chested freshman nobody?' The car hit fifty. 'Aw. You did! How sad.'

Reggie's head spun, the blasting heat suffocating her. 'Stop the car!' she yelled.

The car hit sixty, zooming down the icy road. A few more miles and they'd reach Abernathy Flats, acres and acres of barren, snow-covered farmland. Remote enough for wicked deeds to go unseen and unheard.

Reggie lunged for the steering wheel. The car fishtailed, and the back end lost traction, sending the vehicle into a sickening spin. Quinn swung an elbow hard into Reggie's sternum, and the force of it knocked the breath out of her. She slumped against the window, gasping. Quinn seized the wheel. He steered them out of the three-sixty before pulling over onto the shoulder. The Mustang screeched to a stop.

'Wooooo! Sweet! I *love* this car!'

Reggie opened the door but Quinn grabbed her left wrist.

'Relax. Stay a bit. I said I wanted to talk.'

Where Quinn held Reggie, a chill pierced her, numbing her entire arm.

'Man, was I surprised when I saw that journal you dropped. I knew then I had to keep an eye on you, and I've been trailing you ever since. So when you snuck out to that old house, I followed you. I really thought I'd taken care of you when I torched the place. But surprise, surprise! You got out alive. You're a tough little girl, Reggie Halloway.'

Reggie's gauzed hand ached like sensitive teeth slathered in ice cream. Her fingertips turned purple as Quinn's grip tightened.

'So you know about us. Big deal. That might worry Henry – the *new* Henry – but here's the thing: he's a novice. He's still getting used to his body, his surroundings, how you humans behave. I've been around a lot longer and I don't freak out so easy.'

Reggie shook her head.

'No, no, it can't be, you can't *all* be . . . *Vours*,' she babbled.

'Yeah, that's one name for us, sweetie.' Quinn laughed. 'Creeple, bogeyman, doppelgänger, Vour – take your pick. It's all the same to me.'

Reggie's entire hand was blue now. It looked alien. Dead.

'What do you want?'

'Me? I just want to lead a human life. But something else, something bigger, has plans, Halloway. We "Vours" are just the tip of the iceberg, baby. And the sweetest part of it all? Nobody will see it coming until it's too late.'

'But I know all about you now. And –'

Quinn snapped his gum again. 'You don't know a damn thing.'

His grip tightened on her wrist. Reggie's greying fingers swelled and the skin stretched. She tried desperately to pull away, but his hold was iron.

'But you know what the really scary part is?'

Her fingertips split open and tiny black legs wriggled out.

'The really scary part is now *we know about you*.'

Cackling, he released her as hundreds of black spiders streamed out of her fingers and swarmed up her arm. They raced over her entire body – her eyes, her ears, pouring into her mouth when she tried to scream. Her scrabbling hands found the door handle. She threw open the door, fell out of the car and stumbled into the snow.

'Get them off me!'

Thick strands of spider silk covered her cheeks. She tried to rip them off, but the spiders spiralled their webs faster and faster around her face. They raced around her entire body, cocooning her.

Quinn had shut off the engine to enjoy the show. He leaned back in his seat and had less than a second to brace for impact when a massive SUV slammed into the back of his Mustang. His head smashed against the windshield, splintering the glass and knocking him unconscious.

———

Aaron jumped out of the almost undamaged truck and tackled Reggie in the snow as she tried to free herself from the imaginary spiders. She kicked and screamed at him, ripping into his neck with her nails.

He didn't let her go.

'Reggie! You're okay! Relax. It's me.' Aaron hugged her tight and pressed the side of his face to hers. He whispered in her ear. 'Come back, Reggie. It's okay. It's me, Aaron. I'm here.'

Her spasms slowed. She looked up at him with tear-misted eyes.

'Aaron?'

'Yeah. I'm here.'

She stared at her fingertips and wiggled them. She hugged Aaron back.

'How did – where did –?' she stammered. Above the hum of the engine came muffled shouts from the back of the SUV.

'You weren't outside when I got to your house, so I snuck in. Henry was curled up in front of the TV and I grabbed him. He

162

tried to drown me again but I fought back.' Aaron grinned. 'I pushed back like you did, Reggie. And it worked. I put him in the trunk and waited for you, but –'

'How did you find me?'

'I saw you in Quinn's car when he drove past the house. I followed. Something had to be up, right? Then he swerved and spun out, and I could see you two struggling. You staggered out of the car, and I knew it was my chance to take him out.'

'Yeah. Looks like your mom's yuppie-tank didn't get a scratch, but Quinn –'

Aaron looked into the Mustang and saw Quinn slumped on the steering wheel, blood pouring from a gash in his head. 'This looks bad, Reggie. He needs an ambulance.'

'You want to rescue a Vour?' Reggie asked. 'You're joking, right?'

Aaron gaped at her.

'What? Quinn's one of them? I just thought he was an asshole!'

17

Aaron looked ridiculous behind the wheel of his mom's SUV.

'I don't know how she drives this thing,' he said. 'It's like a yacht. And these seats are worse than my grandmother's sofa. I'm getting sucked in like loose change, and the fuel consumption –'

The grunting and thrashing of the captive in the back interrupted Aaron's rant. He grimaced and shifted in the driver's seat.

'This is messed up,' Reggie said. 'I can't believe we're kidnappers.'

'The Vour is the kidnapper. Not us.'

Open farmland gave over to snow-covered oak and birch that crept right up to the edge of the winding road.

Aaron slowed down, wary that one slip on the icy path could land them in a steep roadside ditch. The SUV crawled through the entrance of the camping grounds surrounding Cutter's Lake.

Reggie stared out of the window. 'Henry created that place – the fearscape – because of *me*.'

'You know that's not true.'

'No? Who left scary movies around for him to watch? Who talks about gruesome, gory legends twenty-four/seven? I mean, what kind of sister reads *horror* books to her brother as bedtime stories? Like the world isn't dark and terrible enough.'

'Most of the world is a good place, Reg.'

'The vampire killer from Sacramento? Jack the Ripper? Dahmer? Bundy? BTK?'

Aaron said nothing. The truck coasted to a halt.

'God, we're monsters. All of us.'

'We all have a dark side, Reggie. You. Me. The old lady down the street. Henry. Everyone. We make the choice not to embrace it, but the dark is there. It's always there. Inside us.'

'Yeah, well.' Reggie opened her door. 'After tonight, I'm only reading cheesy romance novels.'

'Lusty blacksmiths and naughty princesses. Now *that's* scary.' Aaron climbed out of his side. 'We're as close as we can get. I'll leave the headlights on to light our way down to the lake.' He took a tyre iron from the back seat. 'We'll take this to break the ice, okay?'

Reggie didn't answer.

'You can do this, Reg. I know you can.'

'I have to.'

The two stood behind the trunk with a grim determination.

'Open it. Let it out.'

Aaron fumbled with the key and popped the lock. A bluish boy in his underwear lay shivering atop a pile of ice cubes. His hands were bound in front of him. Where the cubes touched his skin, sores bloomed and spread.

'Please . . .' he stammered. 'Reggie . . .'

'Henry . . .' Reggie said softly.

'No,' Aaron snapped. 'This thing is not your brother.'

The boy jerked his head and hissed. Black smoke leaked from his mouth. Aaron reached into the trunk, grabbed Henry by the ankle and yanked him out onto the hard icy ground, where the boy writhed in pain.

166

'*Enough!*' Reggie shouted and shoved Aaron back. She kneeled down beside her brother's body. 'I know you're inside somewhere, Henry. I'm going to find you.'

'So . . . cold . . . scared . . .'

'I know.'

Reggie leaned over him and brushed his forehead. Smoke from his mouth morphed into a spider that leaped at her face. The shock was just enough to freeze her for a moment while Henry scrambled to his feet and staggered towards the woods.

Another set of headlights swung into the parking lot. The car sounded like a low-flying biplane. Its muffler and rear bumper dragged against the road, throwing sparks and clattering.

'Go! Catch Henry and get him in the water!' Aaron handed the tyre iron to Reggie and stuffed some of the ice cubes from the trunk into his pockets. 'I'll deal with this.'

'Aaron –'

'Do it!'

Reggie raced off as the Mustang prowled towards Aaron.

A familiar silhouette lurked behind the cracked, blood-streaked windshield. The car pulled up next to the SUV, and the splintered but functional tail lights of the crushed back end winked out as the car's smooth engine cut off.

The door opened, and Quinn got out. The gash above his right eyebrow had bled all over his leather jacket. One eye had swollen shut.

'You're too late, Quinn. Reggie's got Henry.'

'Really, now. She's your hero, huh?' Quinn walked round the front of Aaron's mom's truck. He shook his head. 'Damn SUVs. You crush my back end but what happens to you? Not even a dented fender. No sense of social responsibility with these things.'

'We've got you figured out, Quinn. Or whatever the hell you are. She knows how to get inside. We know –'

'You don't know shit, pansy.'

Aaron kept his hands in his pockets. The ice cubes had already numbed his fingers. The boys faced each other across the car hood.

'You think your lame girlfriend is some sort of saviour? She wriggles her bony butt inside one little room of our infinite halls and she's your King freakin' Arthur? You know nothing, Cole.'

'I know you're scared of her. I can see your fear.'

Quinn sprang across the hood and pushed Aaron to the ground. He placed a knee on Aaron's chest and a hand to his throat.

'Look in my eyes, boy. Do you see fear?'

Aaron flailed as visions of water rose above his head.

He was drowning.

'Hmm. Guess you do.'

Down, down into the murky depths. The smell of seaweed and the sting of salt. Aaron sank into a dark lagoon. He forgot about Reggie, about Henry, about his family. His flailing stopped, his eyes closed, and his heartbeat slowed.

Aaron started to die.

'I could crush your windpipe with my bare hands,' Quinn said, 'but isn't this more fun?'

———

Catching the monster wasn't hard. It was freezing. It was in agony. And it could only muster enough strength to propel Henry's body thirty metres before finally dropping into a pathetic heap in the snow. Catching it was easy.

Listening to it was torture.

'Reggie,' it said as she scooped the nearly naked child into her arms. 'You're killing me. Can't you see you're killing me? I won't survive the water.'

Reggie closed herself to the mimicked despair. She averted her eyes from the body – the vein-riddled arms and neck, the grotesque black stains across the chest and belly, the white gums. But she couldn't ignore the lethal cold of the skin.

The thing was made of lies. But she worried that it was telling one truth: the water would kill Henry.

The Vour was in the mind, but the body was still mostly human. If Henry's *body* died, if its temperature dropped too low, if its heart stopped pumping, Henry – the *real* Henry – would have nothing to return to. But what other choice did she have?

Reggie carried him down to the bank and stood at the edge of the ice. The headlights above eerily illuminated the lake's frozen surface.

'You're going to murder me, Reggie. Just like in those movies you made me watch. You're a murderer, Reggie. A murderer . . .'

She stepped onto the thick shore ice with her brother's limp body in her arms. A glaze of fresh snow coated the ice and Reggie shuffled forward. The ice at the lake's centre would be thinner.

'Murderer. Mom knew you were sick. That's why she left us.'

'I'm coming for you.' Reggie looked down at her brother's face. 'Whatever the hell you are, I'm coming. And I'm not afraid any more.'

When she reached the middle of the lake, Reggie placed Henry's frail body down. Then she took the tyre iron out of her coat and slammed it into the ice.

'*If you break the ice,*' the boy said in a detached, inhuman voice, '*we all go down. You and Henry will both die.*'

She brought the iron down a second time.

'So be it. We die together.'

'*You really are a stupid one, aren't you, Regina? You and Henry will die.*' The thing chortled. '*I'll be here forever.*'

A third strike knocked a manhole-size hunk of ice loose. Reggie used the tyre iron to prise the chunk out. She grabbed Henry's forearms and dragged him to the hole. By now the boy was so cold he could barely move. Reggie lowered her brother's body, feet first, into the glacial water beneath the ice.

'*Bitch,*' the thing hissed. '*I'm ready for you.*'

The boy's mouth split open into a hideous grin. Black stains now marred bleached gums, and a plume of smoke poured out of its throat. It towered over Reggie, gathering itself into an enormous shadow that eclipsed the distant radiance of the headlights.

The blackness of the monster was all-consuming, deeper than the night that surrounded it. It hung in the sky over the lake for a long moment and then collapsed back into Henry's mouth with a ferocious jolt that almost made Reggie lose her hold on the child.

She yanked her brother's body from the water. His skin now looked charred, ravaged completely, but she did not let herself pity or fear for him. Henry, the real Henry, was locked in some horrible world. She laid the boy's body back on the ice, put her hands to his face, and stared into the wild blue eyes.

'*Come on then, little girl,*' the thing said. '*What are you afraid of?*'

And then Reggie fell for the second time into the black.

18

The carnival expected her.

Reggie awoke in a foetal position. Above her stood a girl holding a pink cotton candy stem in one hand and the freckled boy's severed head in the other. She pressed her foot against Reggie's neck.

'Look who's back,' the girl said as she took a bite of her cotton candy. 'We knew you'd come see us again because –'

'Because you're a moron,' said the skinny kid beside her. He chomped on a long cord of cherry liquorice as he pushed his glasses up his long nose. Thick lenses magnified the dark, bestial eyes behind them. Dozens of children crowded around.

'Right. What he said.' The girl ground her foot into the scabbed slash on the side of Reggie's neck. 'Berzerko was so mad you got away he took it out on this poor kid.' She swung the little boy's head like a toy prize.

The face-painted girl skipped over to them, white larvae dripping from her rotten chin. 'Now that you're back, we're taking you to the Big Top.'

The entire crowd laughed, and Reggie's neck throbbed under

the crushing pressure of the blonde girl's heel. The face-painted girl grabbed Reggie's ankles, and the boy with the glasses tied his liquorice around them. The cord burned into her skin like dry ice. She clenched her teeth and stifled a scream. The stench of her own blistering skin wafted into her nostrils.

The other kids lifted her off the ground. Each ghastly finger that touched her body leaked a bitter and venomous cold that sought to paralyse her.

'To the Big Top! To the Big Top!'

The crowd held her aloft and carried her towards a gigantic, foul-smelling pavilion. Screams and wails poured forth from the evil tent. If she went in, she would never come out again. Inside was pure madness.

She closed her eyes and struggled to calm herself. Reggie's pulse slowed and her mind cleared. The cold burn in her ankles dissipated, and the smell of rotten cherries filled the air.

'Hey!' screamed the boy in glasses. 'What'd you do to my liquorice?'

Reggie's legs broke free. She slammed her right foot forward, caving in the face-painted girl's jaw as if it were papier-mâché. Smoke gushed from the ruin of it, and the girl toppled backwards.

The children gasped and dropped Reggie. She leaped up, shoved past them and ran back to the walkway; through the game booths, the snack huts, the kiddie rides, past the Ferris wheel and the roller-coaster, the log flume and the bumper cars . . .

Reggie cut across the carousel platform to get to the fun house and she could feel the eyes of the beasts behind her. Beneath the calliope's melody, she heard the low growls of hungry things.

The fun house tunnel spun faster now. Reggie tried to run through it, but she lost her balance in the whipping vortex.

Elbows, knees, ankles, head, chin – the tunnel banged her about as she tried to crawl across the slick surface. When she had almost reached the other side, the clown's horn cut the air.

Behind her, at the entrance of the tunnel, she saw the pasty white face, the curly green hair and the blood-spattered suit. Berzerko smiled wide and stepped in, swinging the hatchet in front of him. The swirling tube did not affect him, and he steadily advanced.

Reggie lurched for the edge of the tunnel. Her upper body vaulted over the lip of the cylinder, but her legs twisted up behind her, the force nearly pulling her back inside. With one final lunge, she toppled out onto the chequered floor of the fun house. She rose painfully to her feet and ran into the Hall of Mirrors.

Distorted reflections gave way again to horrific images and fears all around her: glistening spiders, dead loved ones and a newer fear – fire. Her pulse quickened at the sight of flames leaping behind the silvered glass, but Reggie thought only of finding her brother.

'Henry! Can you hear me?' she called out. 'Where are you?'

The scraping noise of a hatchet blade across glass sent her racing deeper into the maze. This time no sawdust signalled the way out. She reached one dead end after another, surrounded by ever more freakish reflections: her father's head served on a platter with an apple in his mouth, her mother rocking a demon infant . . .

Reggie stepped forward, gaping at the images, and felt

something squishy beneath her foot. She glanced down to see that she'd trodden upon a giant red shoe.

The killer clown stood in front of her, his blade at his side. There was no way round him this time, nowhere to run. Mirrors imprisoned her. Desperate, Reggie punched the clown, and her fist sank deep into Berzerko's midsection. The sting of bitter cold raced up her arm and, when she pulled her hand out, her fist was laced with ice. Berzerko raised his hatchet with a gleeful smile. He was invincible in here, here among the mirrors.

The mirrors.

Reggie raised her aching fist and punched again, but this time not at the clown. Instead, she struck the mirror next to him. The glass cracked and the clown stumbled. Reggie's hand bled freely, but she hit the glass again, shattering the mirror. As the glass broke into shards, the clown's make-up cracked, revealing bone beneath the caked greasepaint. Berzerko touched the bone with his gloved fingers like he was trying to plug a breaking dam.

Reggie smashed another mirror and a crevasse split the clown's forehead, pouring smoke. Reggie shoved Berzerko aside, and sprinted down the glass hall towards the arch of light at its end. She heard the shoes flop behind her as she dived out of the house of mirrors.

A soft wind blew her hair, and a light rain fell on neatly mani-cured grass. Flowerbeds lined the road that led uphill into the graveyard. Tears streaked down her cheeks.

Her hands throbbed, and she rubbed them in the cool grass. Any second Berzerko would come charging out of the fun house. Reggie was exhausted; she had to rest for just a minute . . .

But when the clown did not follow, a realization hit her. He couldn't follow. Each environment was contained, a layer with its own boundaries. Henry could cross through.

And so could she.

Reggie now stood at the gates of Cutter's Wedge Cemetery.

At the top of the hill Reggie saw two mourners, dressed in black and huddled together under a black umbrella. She recognized them immediately.

'Mom!' Reggie shouted. 'Dad!'

She sprinted towards them, but they bowed their heads and walked into the thick fog on the edge of the cemetery. By the time she reached the top of the hill, they were gone. Reggie dropped to her knees and read the epitaph carved into the marble headstone.

Henry Thomas Halloway

Beloved Son

Buried on Sorry Night

The last line was scrawled beneath the other two in blood. It was still wet.

'It's not real . . .' Reggie reminded herself, but, even so, she never knew she could feel so sad. She knelt in front of her brother's headstone and began to dig.

She clawed at the ground with her bleeding fingers, trying to ignore the pain. Worms and maggots swarmed up through the dirt and onto her hands, wriggling up her wrists and arms. Reggie fought the urge to retch. She swiped madly at them, and each one she touched turned to a puff of black smoke, but there were always more crawling up through the earth and onto her skin.

Reggie continued to dig, tossing the rocky grave away in chunks. Finally her hands hit something wooden, and she smoothed the dirt away to reveal a casket.

Despite the time-ravaged headstone that marked it, the coffin looked new. She prised the lid open and found Kappy the koala tucked inside, frayed and grubby.

Henry had been here. This was all his mind, his fear. The Vour gave those fears form, but there were some things Henry had shaped too. The coffin belonged to the monster, but the koala belonged to Henry. This gave Reggie some hope, though she realized that if Henry had been carrying Kappy, he had dropped it along the way. How much more would he lose before being lost forever?

'I'm coming,' she whispered to the koala. Reggie climbed inside the coffin and lay on her back.

She shut the lid and clutched Kappy to her chest.

Suddenly, the coffin lurched upwards ninety degrees so that Reggie was in a standing position. A red button with a downward arrow appeared waist high in front of her, and tinny jazz music played softly. A fluorescent light flicked on above her head.

The coffin had transformed into an elevator. It startled her for a moment. But while the environments felt disjointed, she knew now that they tied together around a common theme: Henry's fears.

She pressed the DOWN button and heard the scraping of gears. The car descended, and then the doors opened with a polite *ding*.

Reggie walked out into the sterile hall of a vacant hospital.

'Henry!' she called out. Her voice echoed down the corridor.

The place was eerily silent. No voices, no movement – not even the regulated beeps of heart monitors or the squeaky shuffle of medical carts. She walked to an abandoned, dimly lit nurses' station, where several charts littered the desk. Reggie entered through the swinging door and grabbed one. The letterhead at the top read *St Joseph's Memorial*, a hospital in Boston.

Below that was the patient's name: Henry Halloway.

When he was five, Henry had stayed in the hospital for two weeks to recover from an operation. Reggie had accidentally struck him with a tree branch, and a splinter had lodged in his eye, spread an infection and almost blinded him.

Nothing below the treatment plan on the chart was legible. Reggie picked up a second chart and saw that it was identical to the first. So was the next one. And the next.

She continued down the corridor. Room after room was empty. On one hospital bed she found a small pool of blood spreading across a white sheet. Another room had a set of jagged surgical tools laid out on an operating tray. In this place of Henry's mind, he couldn't conjure the flowers and cards that had decorated his room, the kind nurse that had read to him, the warmth of a loving family that had surrounded him. The Vour forbade her brother's mind to rebuild any memory not steeped in pain and loss.

'So you want pain and loss?' Reggie asked aloud. She armed herself with a long scalpel from the palette. 'You'll get it.'

At a T-junction at the end of the hall, she heard a sucking sound from a small dark room to her right.

'Hello? Is anyone there?' Reggie ran to its door, creaked it open and peered inside.

The light from the hallway spilled across a woman sitting motionless in a rocking chair. She cradled a small, squirming bundle in her arms.

It was feeding.

'Hello?' Reggie's voice sounded thin, like old parchment.

The woman did not answer, but at the sound of Reggie's voice the infant at her breast stopped sucking. Her heart pounded as she fumbled for the light switch and flipped it on.

The mother had been dead for hours, her eyes still open, her tongue hanging out, purple and swollen. But her child had continued to feed, tiny hands scratching at grey, sagging flesh. The baby did not feast on its mother's milk, but on her blood and flesh. With tiny, needlelike fangs, it had bored an apple-sized hole through her chest, and a stream of deep red dripped down the soft rolls of the little creature's chin. The mother's abdomen was ripped open, as if the ravenous offspring had *eaten* its way out of her. What remained of her entrails spilled over her lap and down onto the floor.

As Reggie backed away, the thing continued to turn its neck, following her with its yellow eyes and catlike pupils – twisting, twisting, until the awkward movement put too much pressure on the dead mother's arms; the limbs, stiff from rigor mortis, cracked sickeningly as they unfolded and dropped the naked infant to the floor.

The thing resembled a human baby in both shape and proportion, but its skin was a sickly ash, taut and scaly, and spiky black nubs protruded from the cuticles where nails should be. The child expelled shallow breaths on the floor near its mother's blackening feet, its hours-old arms and legs jerking spastically.

As she watched with morbid fascination, the thing rolled over onto its full belly and slithered across the floor, head craned unnaturally upwards. Reggie heard the thing's tongue suck at the roof of its own mouth, desperate for nourishment. She retreated into the hallway and screamed as pain seared through her foot – another demon baby had plunged its fangs into her ankle, and a dozen more crawled towards her.

Then they were upon her, clawing and biting. Her shrieks echoed off the white walls, but the monsters only delighted in her terror. She swung her scalpel wildly, but the imps were too small and close to the ground to slash without crouching down – which would expose her face and throat to their attacks. Reggie kicked at one, and it skidded across the slick floor. The demon bared its needle teeth and scuttled back towards her.

Reggie felt another spawn sink its fangs into her calf, and she ripped it from her skin, flesh and muscle tearing in hot chunks. Without thinking, she squeezed the back of the creature's neck until the top of its tiny spine popped in her grip. She released the infant monster, but the broken thing rose up unnaturally on its tiny legs, neck askew, and *walked* towards her.

Others bit into her ankles, thighs, back – piercing, biting, *feeding*. The smaller monsters, the runts unable to compete with the stronger ones, lapped frantically at the drops of warm blood that pooled on the floor. Reggie kicked and writhed, knocking the creatures to the floor as she raced down the hall.

The corridor seemed to stretch on forever as she ran, her

breath gasping, the scalpel clutched in her white-knuckled fist. At last, she hazarded a look behind.

The little demons were gone.

Reggie heard raspy breathing coming from behind a nearby door. She entered a room filled with hundreds of white curtained enclosures. The edges of it were steeped in mist. As Reggie approached the first curtain, she heard a child's scream. A tall silhouette holding a needle moved behind the drape.

Reggie yanked back the curtain to find an empty hospital bed with a clean white sheet. Another child shrieked to her left, and the same ominous silhouette loomed behind that curtain. Reggie ripped it aside, but again, no one was there. The piercing wails of boys, girls and infants flooded the room. Reggie ripped curtain after curtain from their metal rungs, always finding an empty bed. The cries grew louder and more pained.

Suddenly Reggie was face-to-face with a surgeon in a grey gown and cap. A surgical mask covered her mouth and nose, and her black eyes leaked streams of smoke. She walked towards Reggie, holding a long needle in one of her latex-gloved hands. She pushed the plunger on the needle, and a stream of acidic green fluid spurted to the ground and sizzled on the tile.

'Time for your shot,' she said.

'Don't come near me.' Reggie wielded the scalpel.

'You're late for your operation. The infection is spreading.'

'What infection?'

'Humanity.' The surgeon's voice was smooth as stainless steel. 'Poisonous. Cancerous. Terminal.'

Reggie sliced at the surgeon, but she stepped effortlessly out of the scalpel's path.

'Very well. I've had more difficult patients. *Security!*'

Two security aides burst from behind the curtains, gorilla-like humanoids with sloping foreheads and dull eyes. Huge biceps and shoulders bulged beneath their grey uniforms. Reggie slashed at them, nicking forearms and fingers, releasing small valves of black steam from their flesh. Undeterred, the aides plodded forward and seized her with their massive hands. She screamed and thrashed as they dragged her back to the operating room. The surgeon and a nurse drifted like ashen ghosts behind them.

The aides heaved her onto the operating table and held her down.

'No!' Reggie writhed and struggled. 'Get off me!'

The surgeon swung a lamp over Reggie's head and flicked on a blinding light, then leaned over her with needle in hand. Reggie let out a ferocious scream and pulled one arm free. She smacked the syringe out of the surgeon's hand, but the nurse grabbed Reggie by the throat and slammed her back onto the table. The two aides pinned Reggie tightly.

A mechanical arm unfolded from underneath the table, whirring and buzzing. Its vice-like metal hand gripped onto her head and held it in place. A small silver tentacle, tipped with a flat disc, slithered from the robotic wrist. Reggie gasped as it swayed in front of her face and placed the metal disc over her right eye. With a click, the disc dilated, opening the eye's lids and holding them in place.

The surgeon bent over her, holding a long gleaming drill.

'We go in through the iris, bore into the lens, through the vitreous until we reach the optic nerve . . .'

'Stop . . . please . . .' Reggie sobbed.

Pure fear overwhelmed her, and the fog at the edge of the room crowded in. She was falling away. She would fail her brother . . .

Then something small and wet touched her left cheek. Reggie strained her eye and saw a twitching nose and whiskers next to her head on the table.

'General Squeak?'

The hamster nuzzled against her, sniffing at the pocket where she had stashed Henry's koala. She began to understand.

Henry had brought the memory of General Squeak to this place, just as he had brought Kappy. These things gave him hope. But the Vour was stripping all of it away until Henry was nothing more than a shadow. Henry had lost Kappy. He had lost Squeak. How much more hope did he have left before he succumbed to this world?

'I won't leave you here, Henry. Not again.'

She stopped kicking and flailing. Her terrified fits only empowered the monster within her brother.

'Do it,' she said. 'Go ahead and carve me up any way you like. I'm not afraid of you.'

The surgeon reeked of raw hatred as she pushed the drill towards the clamp on Reggie's eye. But then her hand shook as if jolted by an electric current. The shaking grew frenzied. The nurse grabbed the surgeon's arm to try to stop the convulsions.

'What's the matter, doc?' Reggie sneered. 'Losing your nerve?'

The surgeon ripped her arm free from the nurse's grip and struck, but not at Reggie. The drill pierced the nurse's left eye and sent a fountain of smoke soaring into the room. The clamp over Reggie's eye withdrew, and the vice holding her head sparked and disengaged. The aides loosened their grips and she broke free, knocking the instrument table over on the floor. Needles, scalpels, drills and clamps splayed onto the tile.

She rolled off the table and raced down the corridor after the fleeing hamster.

Curdling screams from invisible children vibrated inside her bones, but Reggie focused only on the little fur ball.

She turned another dark corner and stumbled into an alcove where white sheets were piled up on the floor against the wall. They turned pink, then darkened to red, then glistened deep crimson.

General Squeak burrowed into the sheets and vanished.

'What –?'

The approaching footsteps echoed in the hall.

Reggie sank her fingers into the blood-soaked linen, gagging against the warm wetness on her skin. She tossed them aside, uncovering a laundry chute built into the wall.

The surgeon rounded the corner. Her mask was gone, and beneath her eyes was only a black pit that billowed smoke. One of her rubber-gloved hands raised a bone saw, and the circular blade whirred to life.

There was no other way out.

Reggie took a deep breath and dived into the chute.

Beneath the roar of the depths, and through the blood ringing in his ears, Aaron heard the sound of laughter. Quinn's laughter.

A Vour's laughter.

He fought to listen. He forced himself to *hear* the monster's cruel delight.

That's it, you bastard. Keep laughing.

Aaron stroked his arms through the water and propelled himself upwards, the pressure in his ears lessening as he rose faster and faster towards the surface. The laughing grew louder and closer, and the smell of bubble gum overpowered the fish and seaweed. He broke the surface of the water in his mind.

Aaron breathed fresh air and recovered himself, but he kept his eyes shut and feigned unconsciousness. Slowly, he reached into his jacket and clutched the ice cubes in his pocket. He just needed to reach Quinn's cheek, his neck – any exposed skin . . .

He swung his arm and pelted Quinn's cheek with ice. Startled, Quinn let go of Aaron and stepped back, but something was wrong. Quinn did not scream in excruciating pain like Henry had done; his skin remained pale but normal-looking.

Quinn felt his cheek and saw the ice on the ground. 'Ice cubes?

What's next on your weapons list, geek? A snow cone?'

Aaron tried to get to his feet, but Quinn pushed him back down.

'Yeah,' Quinn said, wiping water from his face, 'Henry told me about you pelting him with a snowball. Really freaked him out. But, then again, he's just not used to his body yet. Me? I'm much more adapted. See?' Quinn reached down and picked up a handful of snow. He rubbed it across his face without a flinch. 'I've taken worse hits on the football field.'

Aaron noticed that tiny, spidery black lines etched the skin where snow had touched the bloody gash on Quinn's forehead. He curled his fist around a handful of snow.

'The last thing that bitch will see is this face.' Quinn bent over Aaron and stared into his eyes. 'How does that make you feel, hero?'

'Human.' Aaron shoved the snow directly on Quinn's gash, grinding it into the swollen wound. Quinn dropped to the ground, clutching his face.

Aaron stood and kicked Quinn in the side of the head, the toe of his boot clunking against the skull. Quinn lay dazed, but the monster would be on his feet in moments.

On his *feet* . . .

Aaron opened the SUV's door and grabbed a Swiss army knife from the glove compartment. He returned to the Vour moaning on the ground, and yanked off Quinn's shoes and socks, leaving his bare feet exposed. Aaron flicked open the blade and sliced open Quinn's feet, from toe to heel. Quinn screamed as Aaron mashed snow into the cuts.

'You know that expression people use when they get scared,

right?' Aaron stuffed the socks inside the shoes and dangled them by the laces in front of Quinn like dashboard dice. 'They call it *cold feet*.' He hurled the shoes as far as he could into the snowy woods.

'You're done,' Quinn growled. 'You and your girl. Done.'

But Aaron was already racing down to the lake. From the shoreline, he could see the two bodies sprawled at the lake's centre in a serene embrace. Neither Reggie nor Henry moved, but Aaron knew his best friend and her little brother were fighting a battle more harrowing than he dared imagine. He had to reach them before Quinn overcame his temporary handicap.

Aaron stepped out onto the lake. Most of it was covered with white frost, but in a few places the ice was clear, and he could see the deep water below. If the ice cracked, he'd drown for real.

Where could they go that Quinn wouldn't find them? And if Quinn was a Vour, certainly there were others. But how many? Dozens? Hundreds? Thousands?

The headlights of the truck started to dim, the battery draining. Soon the lights would die, and Aaron would be left in pitch black, stranded out on the lake with two comatose bodies and a Vour lurking in the darkness.

The ice crackled on either side of him. He stopped and drew a breath.

They lay just three metres away from him, but to Aaron it might as well have been the other side of a chasm. When he saw the hole in the ice and the dark water that rippled beneath, his knees almost gave out. But the two bodies beside the hole kept him focused.

Reggie had collapsed on top of her brother's body, and her

cheek rested against his chest. Henry, splayed awkwardly beneath her, looked like a character in a demented cartoon. His skin was purple and covered in black splotches. The two small toes on his right foot had turned completely black, and the fingers on both hands were darkening in the same fashion. Vour marks or actual frostbite, Aaron wasn't sure. Henry's tiny frame convulsed in tense, barely perceptible spasms.

His body was dying.

Aaron took off his jacket and tossed it at him, hoping at least to cover Henry's body. The jacket landed more than a foot to the right.

'Good thing you're not my backup quarterback, Cole,' shouted a voice behind him. He looked over his shoulder to see Quinn striding across the ice. 'You throw like a girl.'

Aaron turned to face the Vour. In the dimming light, he saw that the spidery mark above Quinn's eye had spread across the bridge of his nose. The jock had ripped the sleeves from his jacket and pulled them over his bloody feet.

'You're a wuss, you know that, Cole? Always have been, always will be. But you're smart, I'll give you that.' He gestured down at his sliced feet. 'Can't say I saw that one coming. Did your homework.'

'Did yours too. From now on, I don't do research papers for Vour cowards.'

'Cowards, huh? Big talk for a kid afraid of his own bathtub.' The Vour hobbled forward, and the ice cracked and moaned under the weight. Six metres separated them now.

'Yeah, well. Come any closer and we'll all take a bath.'

Quinn limped towards Aaron and the ice crackled again. A

single, thin rift formed between the two of them.

'*I can smell your fear.*' The sarcasm vanished from Quinn's voice. Pure monster spoke now, a second raspy tone echoing behind Quinn's own. '*Ever smell a rose, Aaron? Really smelled it? Put your nose into the petals and breathed it in? The aroma is intoxicating. Do you know why?*'

The Vour limped forward again. The ice crunched beneath its feet.

'*Because if you bury your nose deep and breathe through the life of a rose, through the flesh and the earth and the beauty, you smell the death inside.*' The Vour breathed deeply. '*It doesn't think, not like humans, but it feels. It feels the end of its life looming almost as soon as it blossoms. And it fears. A rose's perfume is the terror of its own approaching death. I smell that on you tonight. Thick as blood.*'

Aaron stepped backwards and heard the ice start to give way behind him. The headlights faded and died.

20

The dark chute extended for a hellish eternity. Reggie's mind raced through a catalogue of things her brother had been afraid of, and she tried to predict the next layer in this volatile landscape. Would she plummet into some psychotic jailhouse packed with mutant inmates? Splash down in the middle of a black ocean filled with giant sharks? Henry was a little boy; the possibilities were numerous.

Without warning, the chute opened up and Reggie plunged from a vent onto a huge mess of ladies' footwear. She let out a grunt as the heel of a brown leather boot pressed into her stomach.

This wasn't quite the hell she'd expected.

She lifted her shirt and examined the red indent, and then chucked the heeled boot across a drab but cluttered stockroom. As she waded through hundreds of shoes, she mused for a moment about eternal damnation amid stiletto heels, riding boots and smelly cross-trainers.

General Squeak scuttled out of the pile and up Reggie's shirt. He hid in her collar as she walked past row after row of shoeboxes. Like the hospital, this place felt hopeless and forsaken. She lifted the lids of a few boxes, but found nothing but shoes inside.

She moved out onto the sales floor of a department store. Reggie knew this place: the ladies' shoe department on the second floor of the Burlington Mall, where Mom took them shopping for school clothes each August. But what frightened Henry about the mall?

As she walked out of the shoe displays and into Women's Apparel, the racks of clothes began to grow. They groaned and stretched like metal oaks until they towered over Reggie in a twisted, menacing forest, and the scent of sweet perfumes drifting from the cosmetics area turned rank. The pulsing black fog that encased the surreal department store crept in between the grotesque mannequins and mammoth clothing racks, shrouding the world in a suffocating mist.

Henry was close. He had to be.

Nothing else could explain the transformation that took place before her eyes. While the carnival and the cemetery had changed between Reggie's jaunts into the fearscape, this place morphed fluidly. Henry's fear was peaking here, and that fear was reshaping the world around them. *Why is he so scared of this place?*

Then the memory hit her.

When Henry was four, they'd been shopping at the mall, and Mom and Reggie had turned round in a crowd to find Henry gone. They'd searched everywhere, racing around, yelling his name. Reggie had found him hidden in a rack of wool overcoats in the men's department, curled up and paralysed. He was sobbing.

'*Mom lost me . . . she lost me . . . she lost me . . . she lost me . . .*'

And now they were back here, and Mom was really gone. Wrenched out of their lives like a limb torn from the socket.

'Regina.' A voice echoed through the mist. A calm, familiar voice . . .

Reggie could just make out the curves of the escalator railings and a figure that rode up the stairs from the lower level. She recognized the silhouette before the entire body rose into view.

Mom.

Reggie's impulse was to run through the mist and embrace the beautiful woman, to feel the ticklish warmth of Mom's long hair as it brushed her cheeks. But the temperature of the air on the second floor dropped instantly. Frost caked the metal clothing racks as a deadly chill blew through the fog. This thing was not her mother.

'Regina?' it called, mimicking Mom's kind voice. 'Are you up here, honey? I was told you'd be coming to see me.'

Reggie darted behind a mannequin display and watched the woman walk towards the shoe department, the heels of her elegant shoes clacking in steady cadence across the marble floor. The mannequin's head turned atop the motionless body. Glowing eyes stared down at Reggie.

'Uh-oh,' Mom said. She stopped and turned round. 'Are you hiding from me, Regina?'

The mannequin turned at its waist on the pedestal, plastic limbs creaking and reaching out for Reggie. She staggered back as more groans and cracks echoed through the gloom. Every mannequin in the store had turned to face her. They stared down from their platforms, eyes gleaming on expressionless faces.

'I see you, dearest,' the mother-thing called from the shadows.

The mannequins broke from their moorings and stepped down onto the floor.

Reggie stumbled half blind through the congealing fog towards the escalator. Mom's heels clicked evenly through the mist behind her. At the top of the moving stairs, Reggie tripped and fell, tumbling down to the bottom of the escalator. The lower level of the store was choked in a black, miasmic film.

There was no up, no down.

There was only the dark.

'Henry?' she called out into the black. 'Henry, can you hear me?'

From a nearby rack of clothing, she heard muffled sniffling. Reggie ran to the rack and pulled two wool coats apart. Beneath them, curled up in a trembling ball, was Henry.

Reggie swelled with love as she crawled underneath the rack.

'Hey, little man,' she said gently, reaching out a hand to stroke his soft hair. 'I found you.' She leaned in slowly and kissed his cheek – he was warm, soft and good. 'I'll always find you.'

The boy trembled at her touch.

'Talk to me, Henry. Tell me you can hear me.'

'You're not Reggie,' he whispered. 'You're a monster. You're all monsters here.'

He clutched a photograph to his chest. It was the picture of their family at the carnival: Henry, Reggie, Dad and Mom. It was his final sliver of hope, the one bread crumb he refused to leave behind.

General Squeak's whiskers tickled the back of Reggie's neck. He scurried down her arm and onto Henry. The boy watched the hamster's movement and a smile crept across his face. Reggie pulled the koala from her pocket and held it out to her brother.

'I'm real, Henry. And General Squeak is real. And Kappy. We're going to get you out of here.'

'What about Mom? Will Mom come with us? When will she come home?'

'I . . .' Reggie wanted to comfort him, to lie to him, but did not. The fearscape was built out of lies, and she would not feed it. 'I don't know, Henry. I know I act like I've got it all figured out, but I don't. Mom left us, and I don't know why. I wish I could tell you that it will be better –' her voice cracked – 'but she's gone, Henry. She's gone and I don't know if she's ever coming back.'

'Doesn't she love us any more?'

'I –' Reggie choked on her words. 'I don't know. But I love you, Henry. I'll always love you. And I'll never leave you again.'

Henry lunged for Reggie and squeezed her tight. Warmth flooded from the little boy and filled Reggie with strength. 'I want to go home.'

'Oh, you are home, my sweet boy.' Mom's voice cut from behind a rack of coats and through the darkness. 'You are home with Mommy, right where you belong.'

21

A large chunk of ice broke away right behind Aaron, and he slipped to his knees.

'I just wanted to drown you in fear, Cole,' Quinn said in his human voice. 'But it looks like you've opted for the real deal, huh?' He laughed and shook his head. 'What a story this will make.'

Aaron struggled to stay atop a wobbly hunk of ice. The fissures widened around him.

'"Troubled Teen Drowns Girlfriend, Then Self",' Quinn continued. 'Now that's a gripping headline. Cutter's Wedge folks don't get the juicy homicide/suicide stories like the big cities, Cole. You'll be the talk of the town for years!'

Aaron crawled towards the bodies on the adjacent plate of ice.

'They'll interview your parents, your teachers . . . they'll snoop through your locker and your bedroom. Wonder what they'll find.'

Aaron crept across the deepening cracks in the ice and reached his friends. He put his hand on Reggie's back. She was still breathing, still alive. Still in the fearscape with Henry.

Henry felt like a corpse to Aaron's touch. He gripped the boy's ankle tightly and, on hands and knees, pulled the entwined siblings inch by inch to the shore. Quinn took another step forward, just as wary of the splitting ice as Aaron.

'You won't make it to the other side without those two coming apart,' Quinn said.

'Maybe not. But I'll get them both to safety.'

'Safety? Not much of a girlfriend if her brain's cooked.'

So, if Reggie and Henry's physical contact was broken during the trance, she might not ever come back . . .

'Good to know, Quinn. Thanks for the tip.'

'Doesn't matter what you know. You're dead.'

Aaron stood up, took hold of Henry's ankle again, and shuffled towards shore. A few steps across, the ice shifted and upset his balance. He dropped Henry's ankle to brace a palm against the ice. His left hand touched down on metal instead. It was the tyre iron he'd given Reggie to make the hole.

'We've taken your girlfriend.' Quinn circled the breaking section of ice, puffs of black smoke rising from his eyes and mouth and writhing in the air like snakes. 'We've taken her little brother. And we've taken more. So many more.'

Aaron picked up the tyre iron and wobbled to his feet. He'd dragged Reggie and Henry almost four metres from the hole. Not far, but far enough away from the thinnest ice. The portion beneath his feet felt thicker, if just barely so. It could hold a few minutes, but not if Quinn came closer. Not if Aaron didn't make a move.

He charged at Quinn, full of rage, and brought the tyre iron down hard and fast. Quinn raised his right arm to shield the blow, and the rod hit it just below the elbow. The monster shrieked, cradling his forearm, but Aaron did not relent. He dived at Quinn, and the two fell down hard onto the ice. The lake cracked under Quinn's back and a spurt of water splashed over both of them.

Aaron lifted the tyre iron again. His body shook from the chill of the frigid water. But as he brought the rod down a second time, Quinn punched him in the throat.

Aaron gagged and bit his tongue. He dropped the tyre iron and rolled sideways, clutching his windpipe and gasping for breath. Quinn picked up the tyre iron in his left hand. The other arm hung limply at his side.

'You psycho,' Quinn said, waving the iron slowly. 'You have any idea how lucky you are that this isn't my throwing arm?'

He pierced Aaron's shoe with the sharp end of the iron. Aaron croaked in pain as new veins cracked across the ice. Quinn grabbed the tyre iron with both hands and held it over Aaron's chest, point downward, like an impaling spike.

'I am *so* tempted to stab you through the heart. *But* you need to make a pretty corpse so that when they drag you from the lake, it just looks like your girl put up a good fight.'

He lifted Aaron's bleeding foot and dragged him towards the fresh crack in the ice.

'So now, you drown.'

With his uninjured leg, Aaron swiped at Quinn's ankles and knocked his feet out from underneath him.

Quinn crashed through a patch of thin ice and fell into the freezing water. He clawed at the slippery ice, sliding down into the water until only his head and arms remained above the surface. Aaron, still on his back, was afraid to stand up; he was terrified that the ice would give way beneath him. He tried to roll away from Quinn, but a flailing hand caught hold of his ankle and held fast. Quinn was sinking, and dragging Aaron down with him.

Aaron kicked at the clutching fingers, and desperately struggled for a handhold on the ice, but it was of no use. He slid helplessly on his back towards the blackening Vour, the dark water and death.

22

Reggie flung the coats on the rack wide open and stared up at the monster that had taken the form of her mother.

'Regina Marie Halloway.' She put her hands on her hips, then she smiled, and Reggie heard the crackle of ice. 'Just what do you think you're doing under there?'

Henry ducked behind his sister, desperately trying to hide.

'Henry?' Mom said. 'I'm ashamed of you. We talked about visitors down here, didn't we? Do you remember what Mommy said about inviting –'

'Shut your hole,' Reggie said. 'I don't need an invitation. I know how this game of yours works now, and I'm taking my brother back.'

Mom reached out a smooth, dainty hand. 'Now, I won't ever claim to be the perfect mother, Regina.' Her arm stretched like toffee and clutched Reggie by the throat. She yanked her out from under the rack. 'But I deserve respect in my household.'

Henry scrambled out. 'Don't hurt her, Mama!'

Mom's face contorted into a gruesome mask with cheeks stretched upwards, eyes bulging. Her skin rippled violently as she pointed a long finger at Henry.

The boy's mouth disappeared; from nose to chin, there was only a smooth plane of skin.

'Quiet, Henry dear.'

Reggie scratched at the cold grip on her throat.

'Fight her . . .' Reggie choked.

Mom's arm reeled Reggie in. The girl wriggled her feet and gasped for breath as the fog closed in again.

'I don't know how you got this far,' Mom whispered, 'but you've failed. And once you're gone I am going to torture your little brother in ways you can't fathom. And it will never end –'

As Reggie hung helplessly in the air, General Squeak scuttled up the mother's long skirt and then climbed onto her back. Reggie craned her head and caught a glimpse of Henry.

Now, instead of fear, his face was twisted with anger. His mouth rematerialized on his face.

'Put her down,' the boy said. 'Don't you dare hurt my sister.'

Mom's eyes widened as the rodent scuttled down her outstretched arm.

'Tell it to get off me.' Mom's head twisted completely around. 'Tell it to get down, or I'll rip her head clean off.'

'No,' Henry replied. 'I said, put her down!'

The hamster sank his teeth deep into the monster's wrist, tearing a long gash down her arm. Mom shrieked as black smoke poured from the gaping wound. Reggie prised the icy fingers from her neck and dropped to the ground.

She staggered to her feet and raced for her brother, who now just stared at the wailing vision of their mother.

'Come on, Henry. Let's go!' She pulled him to the escalator, and the moving steps quickly carried them away. When they reached the top, they stood in the cold hallway of the hospital. The escalator behind them vanished, leaving only a wall of mouldering white tile in its place.

A crowd of children rounded the corner at the hallway's opposite end and shambled towards them. Grey-skinned and blank-eyed, they wore tattered hospital gowns and suffering expressions. They were dead, but they walked, their wounds leaking vile fluids.

Reggie took Henry's trembling hand.

'Don't be afraid. They're not real. Just follow me, and walk through them.'

They waded through phantoms. With mournful cries, the children reached out with tiny dead hands for the siblings. Henry clung to his sister, trying to look straight ahead.

'Don't go, Henry,' one of them mewed.

'Stay. Don't leave us,' begged another.

The children's sadness churned into anger.

'No way out,' one hissed. Another echoed the words. 'No way out.' More and more voices shouted. 'No way out! No way out!'

'Come on!' Reggie urged.

Reggie and Henry raced through the crowd, scrambling down hall after hall, but there was no sign of an exit; every turn brought them face-to-face with a horde of ghouls. Then they heard the click-clacking of heels approaching.

The ghouls drew nearer. The clacking grew louder, but Henry could not move.

'Henry, they're not real! It's your *fear* that's real! Do you understand? That's why we're still trapped here! The Vour thinks you're just a scared little kid!' Reggie took her brother by the shoulders. 'Aren't you tired of being scared?'

'Yes.'

'So don't be,' she said. 'There's an elevator here somewhere. Where is it, Henry?'

One little girl reached for Henry and her spectral form passed through him. Henry cried out.

'You just have to calm down long enough to see it! These ghosts can't hurt you!'

Henry clutched his sister's hand and shut his eyes. The ghouls pushed forward, but broke against the boy's small body like a wave.

'That's it, Henry. Show this thing it can't scare you any more.'

The ghosts halted, as if an invisible fence stood between them and their prey. Suddenly, the elevator appeared.

'Good job.'

23

Quinn was submerged save for a blistered arm, bent at the elbow and resting flat against the ice. He gripped Aaron's ankle with the assuredness of death.

Aaron screamed. He howled himself hoarse, his terrified gaze leaping to the silent shapes of Reggie and Henry, then to the dark water. Quinn outweighed Aaron by at least fifteen kilos. He would sink – and pull his captive along with him. Aaron sat up, clawing and beating the hand, but it would not let go . . .

Light shone across the lake. Aaron looked over to the parking lot to see a pair of headlights gleam back at him.

Aaron skidded on his butt another half a metre towards the frigid water. He flopped back down on the ice. More surface area spread across the ice was less likely to break it. And there was nothing harder to move than dead weight. *Dead weight.* He prayed that he wouldn't die this way.

A figure, silhouetted by the headlights, made its way across the lake. It moved carefully but quickly.

The ice cracked around the hole, the sound like a cable snapping. Aaron screamed for Reggie, for Henry, for the person on the lake, for God, for anyone. No one answered.

The figure drew closer, taking deft, precise steps over the cracked ice. It balanced itself with a cane.

Aaron slid again, and his legs were dragged into the water. The monster seized his belt, trying to pull itself up, but instead pulling Aaron deeper into the ice hole.

There was a dark blur across Aaron's vision; it took him a moment to make out the familiar face.

'Eben . . . how?'

The old man set his cane to one side, bent over in a wide stance, and with nimble fingers unbuckled Aaron's belt. Under Quinn's weight, the belt slipped its loops, and Eben yanked Aaron back from the water. He was free.

Eben snatched Quinn's hand by its wrist and pulled.

'No!' Aaron shouted. 'He's one of them!'

Quinn broke the water's surface, now only a semblance of what he was before. Sheets of wrinkled and blackened skin hung from his face and arms. Eben held him up by the wrist, viewing him not with horror, or fear, or any visible emotion at all; he looked like a fisherman unimpressed with his catch.

The oozing, blistered face stared back at Eben.

'*You,*' the Vour said, its voice like a warped cello. '*We killed you a long time ago.*'

Eben said nothing. In a single twisting motion, he snapped the wrist like dry kindling, and then he let go.

The Vour opened his mouth wide and smoke poured out in place of a scream. It seeped from his eyes and nostrils and stretched out above his head. The monster dwarfed the size of the Vour in the basement, a shadow blacker than deep space. It smothered Aaron and Eben, wrapping wispy talons round their necks, but the Vour itself had no physical strength.

The spirit stretched and twisted, tethered to the sinking body like a vile kite.

A lucid look flashed across Quinn's face. 'Aaron?' he whispered. And then he went under, dragging the Vour behind him, down into the icy water.

Coughing, Eben stooped to pick up his cane. When Aaron met his eyes, they held a depth, or perhaps a coldness, like he'd never witnessed before. He felt the man's smile in his stomach.

'What are you doing here? How did you know –'

'Hold your tongue and get on your feet, Mr Cole. We still have some work to do.'

24

Reggie and Henry ran inside the elevator, but still the clack of heels neared, and ice began to coat the inside of the compartment. Henry pushed the button, but his finger stuck to the frozen surface. Mom appeared at the other end of the dark hospital corridor.

'Running away from home? Shame on you.'

Reggie pounded the button. The frosty doors closed with a splintering groan. The car raced up and then fell backwards. Both Henry and Reggie slammed against the wall just as the corny jazz music cut out and the elevator lights popped. The worms and maggots broke through the rotting coffin and leached onto them, swelling fat and thick on Henry's mounting fear.

'Don't let them scare you. Use them!' Reggie shouted. 'Command them. Make them dig us out. You said you were tired of being afraid. Get us out of here! Do it!'

Henry closed his eyes. She felt the worms struggle, fighting his will with a fierce determination. It was one thing for Reggie to defeat the fear in this place, but for Henry to conquer it was another game entirely.

'Dig,' Henry said. '*Dig us up!*'

Reggie felt the earth and wood dissolve away around them. The worms were obeying. Within moments they were cracking the weedy surface and crawling out from the ground.

But so were all the other bodies in Cutter's Wedge Cemetery. All around them corpses broke through the soil. Some bodies were covered in decomposing flesh and ragged dresses, recent residents in the graveyard. Others were bone and wiry hair.

'Damn it, Henry! Cut it out!' Reggie pulled her brother out of the grave and dragged him down the slope towards the mirrors. 'Your fear is making this worse! Calm down, damn it!'

'You swore, Reggie! Twice!'

Reggie shouldered and shoved her way through the undead hordes, her willpower causing them to collapse and crumble at her touch. Henry followed close at her heels, amazed at his sister's strength.

They ran into the Hall of Mirrors at the bottom of the hill just as Mom rose from the earth of Henry's grave. Inside, horrible reflections played out on the evil mirrors as they stumbled back through the maze towards the carnival.

'Don't watch,' Reggie said, knowing it was impossible to turn away. 'Don't fear this place!'

They emerged from the mirrors, dashed through the spinning cone and out of the fun house.

'How did you get here, Henry?' Reggie demanded. 'Where did you come in?'

'Over there,' said Henry, pointing across the carnival grounds to the red turnstile Reggie had entered on her first visit. She nodded.

'Then that's how we're getting out.'

They hopped up onto the carousel to cut across towards the carnival entrance. As Henry passed, horrible metallic groans cried out to him. The hideous beasts on the ride tore away from the carousel platform. Winged gargoyles, demons and nightmare horses wrenched free from the metal poles and chased Reggie and Henry down the walkway. Children with smoking eyes cheered and whistled from all sides.

'Hey, it's scaredy cat and his loser sister!' shouted the boy in thick glasses. 'Where ya goin', scaredy cat?'

'You guys better quit clowning around!' jeered the blonde girl, her head still caved in. 'Berzerko's hopping mad at you now!'

They could see the entrance and the red turnstile that marked the edge of Henry's fearscape, but before they could reach it they heard the blare of the air horn. Berzerko hopped onto the walkway. He blocked the way out.

Behind, the gargoyles and demons bore down on them in a screeching swarm of teeth, horns and wings. One of the gargoyles snatched Reggie in its talons and pinned her to the sawdust-coated ground. It grinned with teeth of pointed stone and drooled grey slime on her forehead.

Henry stood in the centre of the walkway, half frozen. The children hooted and clapped until an angry roar silenced them all.

'*Insolent brats!*'

All the fiendish children cowered. The carousel demons went fearfully still, and even the clown dared not move. One fear permeated them all. One fear ripped across all boundaries and flooded over this entire world, briefly freezing time itself.

Mom.

She limped down the walkway towards Henry, a broken-heeled shoe in her remaining hand.

'I've tried to be a good mother, Henry.' With each step, the ground behind her iced over. 'But you just refuse to be a good son. Look at all the trouble you've caused.' She lifted up her blackened arm. 'And you wonder why I left you?'

'Henry!' Reggie blurted. 'Don't listen to that thing!'

The gargoyle on top of Reggie dug its claws into her chest and she screamed in agony. Now, instead of blood, black smoke poured out of her. She was becoming a part of this place. They needed to get out now, before it consumed both of them.

The deranged clown loomed behind her brother, but in front of him stood a fear so much closer to his heart. He faced the foreboding that crossed all boundaries, the dread that could cut him deeper than any blade.

'Come along, Henry.' The monster dropped the shoe and raised its hand to his cheek. 'Come home with Mommy.'

Henry took the photograph out of his shirt pocket.

'You left us,' he said through flowing tears.

'Of course I did, you little toad. You and your useless sister drove me away. I couldn't stand to be around either of you a day more. All you did was complain. All you did was want. All you did was take.'

'It's not your fault, Henry.' Reggie's voice was barely louder than a puff of smoke.

'What if it was my fault?' cried Henry.

Mom's mouth spread into a cavernous black hole. The gaping maw was like a dark cyclone, poised to pull him in. The air swirled furiously. Reggie thought she could feel bits of herself tearing away, disappearing into the void of the fearscape. Henry was losing.

'I think she did her best to take care of us, Henry,' she whispered. 'But something happened inside her. Something made her feel like all she could do was run away.'

Mom towered over the boy, and the ground around them turned to ice.

'Mom wasn't brave enough, Henry,' said Reggie. 'She was the one who was scared. She couldn't face her fear. Not you. You stand up to it. We practised together, remember?'

That conversation they'd had on Henry's bed seemed ages ago now. Could Henry even recall it?

'That's right, we practised,' said Henry slowly, as if digging up a memory long buried. He turned to his sister and spoke so softly. 'I believe you, Reggie.'

Behind Henry, Berzerko raised the hatchet. The red-slick blade shone in the dull light before it came swinging down.

The boy gazed at the photograph of his family, the last vestige of love and warmth.

'I love you, Mommy, but we'll be all right without you.'

The distorted image of his mother leaned forward, ready to swallow Henry whole, just as the hatchet sailed through the air. Berzerko's blade sheared into her neck and passed clean through. Chocolate hair twirled and danced like ribbons in the breeze as her head tumbled, severed, to the ground.

'Oops,' said the boy in the glasses. 'I think he missed.'

The clown stumbled backwards, smoke wafting from his eyes and mouth. He shook as if being electrocuted and then vanished into a column of golden flames. Only the hatchet-hand remained, lying on the ground and smouldering. Soon it disappeared as well.

The gargoyle on Reggie exploded into white powder. All around her, creatures and children crackled and burst into brilliant flashes of white. The rides quavered and imploded into tiny suns, and the ice and sawdust beneath them turned to cottony down. A deafening roar shook the world as Mom's body swirled like oily paint down a storm drain. Soon only Reggie, Henry and the red turnstile remained on the emptied fearscape's canvas.

Reggie threw her arms round her brother. 'You did it, Henry. You battled your worst fears. And you *won*.'

For a moment he hung limp in her arms, and then he hugged her back. Exhausted, they walked to the turnstile.

'Henry,' Reggie said. 'I need to tell you something before we go. Our bodies may still be in danger. We might –'

'It's okay,' said Henry. 'Whatever happens, I'm not scared.'

'Me neither.' Reggie gestured to the turnstile, catching just the slightest whiff of buttered popcorn. 'After you.'

Henry pushed through the turnstile and Reggie followed.

The entire fearscape collapsed behind them.

25

Reggie gasped and moaned on the ice.

'Reggie!' Aaron shouted. 'Reggie! Are you alive?'

The black fog of her mind cleared away, and the frigid air jolted Reggie back into reality. She opened her eyes.

'I'm alive.'

'We won't be for long if we stay on this lake,' Eben said.

'Henry.' Reggie struggled onto her knees and looked down at her brother. The mottled burns on the boy's face and body had faded to mere bruise-like shadows, but the whole of him now looked bluish and he shivered wildly. Some of his fingers and toes were black. 'Oh, my God,' she gasped.

Eben took off his wool overcoat and wrapped it around Henry. 'I've got your brother.'

'Eben! What are you doing here?'

'We will talk another time,' he said. 'This boy needs medical attention *now*.'

Henry's eyes popped open, dilated and uncomprehending. As Eben lifted him up, the boy's shivering lessened, but his breathing seemed even shallower.

'Hold on, Hen,' Aaron said. 'We'll get you all warmed up.'

Hobbling with his cane tucked under his arm, Eben carried Henry to shore. The child hung limply in his arms. Aaron put on his jacket, and then he and Reggie staggered behind, supporting one another.

'Get him in the truck.' Aaron stumbled beside Reggie up the bank. 'I have supplies.'

He dragged a duffel from the trunk as Eben laid the boy across the SUV's back seat. The old man untied Henry's bonds. Before Aaron could speak, Reggie snatched the bag from him and frantically pulled towels and blankets from it. A hot-water bottle tumbled onto the ground.

'He's blue.' A twinge of hysteria creaked in her voice.

'He's cyanotic from exposure. Be calm,' Eben said. 'Dry him gently.'

Eben wrapped up the hot-water bottle and placed it on the child's chest while Aaron swaddled the darkening hands and feet with dry towels. Reggie cocooned her brother with quilts. He remained still as a corpse.

'Henry.' Reggie leaned over him, stroking his hair. 'Henry, we made it. Please!'

The boy took a huge shuddering breath, then stirred.

'Reggie,' he said, his tiny voice sleepy and slurred.

'Yes.' Tears misted her eyes. 'I'm here.'

'The Vour poured out of him while he was still knocked out on the ice,' Aaron said, placing his hand on her shoulder. 'It just . . . vanished. You beat it.'

'I didn't beat it, Aaron. Henry did.'

Henry closed his eyes again and drifted off, but his breathing steadied, and his colour returned. Eben crouched to examine him. The tip of Henry's left ear was burned black.

'We need to get to a hospital,' he said.

'Eben. Please tell me what you're doing here.'

'He saved me, Reg,' Aaron said quietly. 'He stopped Quinn.'

Eben stood slowly. His face was granite. His long shadow spilled across her, cast by the Cadillac's headlights.

'I'd hoped it wouldn't come to this. But events have unfolded in a way I did not foresee.'

'Who the hell are you?' Reggie backed away, the man she once saw as a second father now an intimidating stranger.

'I'm an old soldier fighting a war you're just beginning to understand.'

'God,' Aaron said flatly. 'You knew. The entire time you knew. Why –'

'Listen to me very carefully,' Eben continued. 'The battery is dead on this monstrosity.' He pointed at the SUV. 'I'll jump-start it with my car. But hear me now, both of you.' Eben pointed into the night sky beyond the lake. 'Do you see that cluster of stars over there?'

A single asterism burned brighter than the rest, shimmering like a handful of blue sapphires.

'What?' Aaron asked. 'You mean the Pleiades?'

'Very good. I figured you'd be interested in astronomy. The Pleiades cluster is at its most visible now.'

'Have you lost your mind?' Reggie snapped. 'Why should we care about that right now?'

'Because,' Eben said, 'that's what you all came out here to see, away from the lights of town, out on the lake's wide-open space.

215

But poor Henry fell through the ice, so you got him out of his wet clothes, wrapped him in a blanket and rushed him to the ER. That's your story. Do not waver from it.'

'What about Quinn's car?' Aaron asked.

'I'll take care of it. I know a thing or two about making people disappear. Now move.'

———

Reggie sat in the back of the SUV, cradling her shivering brother. She'd cast aside the wet and unravelling bandages from her hands. Black lesions criss-crossed her knuckles where the mirrors had cut her, and her shoulder burned from the gargoyle's talons. She looked at her reflection in the window glass. A knit cap covered her charred hair, and dark rings encircled her eyes.

Henry was safe. Nothing else mattered.

Aaron turned the key in the ignition and the engine roared. It took only seconds before blasts of heat filled the interior. Eben turned from them and slipped into the dark night.

'Where's Quinn?' Reggie asked. 'What happened to him?'

'He's . . . gone.'

Aaron reminded himself that Quinn had tried to kill him – that he was a Vour – but he couldn't help thinking about the real Quinn, the Quinn trapped in his own horrific world for years longer than Henry. And he wondered just how on earth they would explain the death of their town's golden boy.

Reggie nodded. 'Get us to the emergency room. Hurry.'

Aaron spun the truck round and drove towards the few remaining lights that shone in the sleepy town.

'The world of Cutter's Wedge still spins, Reggie. I didn't think you'd make it back. I thought you were both lost.'

Reggie kissed her brother's head and caressed the blackened pinkie finger on Henry's right hand.

'He's a tough kid, Aaron.'

'Like his sister.'

The bright red cross that marked the C. W. Hospital Emergency Entrance came into view as Aaron pulled into the circular driveway.

Reggie opened the door and stepped out. She lifted Henry up in her arms and kicked the door shut with her foot. Aaron rolled down the passenger side window.

'Go,' she said. 'Find Eben. And call my Dad. Tell him . . . tell him we need him.'

'Reggie?' Aaron's voice was dour. 'Quinn told me there were more of them. A lot more.'

'Quinn's dead now. So is the Vour in the basement. And so is the monster that took Henry. We survived.'

Even as she said it, she remembered the hideous voice that had groaned from her brother's lips: '*I'll be here forever.*'

'But they'll come for us again,' Aaron said. 'They'll come for you.'

Reggie carried her brother towards the white, warm light of the emergency room lobby as a gentle snow began to fall. Eben had said that this was a war, one she was only beginning to understand . . . and he was right.

'They'll come.' She did not turn round. 'I'll be ready.'

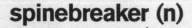